"911. What's your emergency?" a competent-sounding voice answered.

Franny rattled off her address. "Send the police, please. Someone's being...kidnapped, I guess? Forced out of the building and she's fighting back."

"Who? Can you give me a name?"

"No, I don't know who. It's too dark, but she's fighting him." Franny made it to the bottom of the stairs. "They're in the parking lot behind the bakery, the address I gave you."

"And where are you?"

"I saw it through my apartment window. I ran downstairs—"

"Ma'am, I'm going to need you to remain inside. I'm dispatching a deputy to the address. You need to stay inside. Do you understand?"

But Hope Town was so isolated. How long would it take for a deputy to get here? The woman was being dragged to the car now.

Franny looked down at her bat, the woman in her ear just a buzzing now. She clicked End on the call. She didn't want to do anything stupid, but how could she just let someone be taken against their will?

EYEWITNESS IN DANGER

NICOLE HELM

INTRIGUE

For Franny and my allergy boys.

Recycling programs for this product may not exist in your area.

ISBN-13: 978-1-335-69051-7

Eyewitness in Danger

For questions and comments about the quality of this book, please contact us at CustomerService@Harlequin.com.

Harlequin Enterprises ULC
22 Adelaide St. West, 41st Floor
Toronto, Ontario M5H 4E3, Canada
www.Harlequin.com

HarperCollins Publishers
Macken House, 39/40 Mayor Street Upper,
Dublin 1, D01 C9W8, Ireland
www.HarperCollins.com

Printed in Lithuania

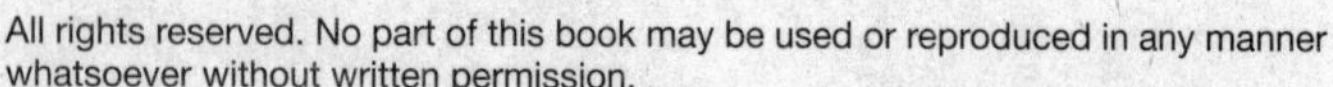

Nicole Helm grew up with her nose in a book and the dream of one day becoming a writer. Luckily, after a few failed career choices, she gets to follow that dream—writing down-to-earth contemporary romance and romantic suspense. From farmers to cowboys, Midwest to *the* West, Nicole writes stories about people finding themselves and finding love in the process. She lives in Missouri with her husband and two sons, and dreams of someday owning a barn.

Books by Nicole Helm

Harlequin Intrigue

Bent County Protectors

Vanishing Point
Killer on the Homestead
Fatal Deception
Eyewitness in Danger

Hudson Sibling Solutions

Cold Case Kidnapping
Cold Case Identity
Cold Case Investigation
Cold Case Scandal
Cold Case Protection
Cold Case Discovery
Cold Case Murder Mystery

Covert Cowboy Soldiers

The Lost Hart Triplet
Small Town Vanishing
One Night Standoff
Shot in the Dark
Casing the Copycat
Clandestine Baby

Visit the Author Profile page at Harlequin.com.

CAST OF CHARACTERS

Royal Campbell—Deputy with the Bent County Sheriff's Department. Patrolling Hope Town when a kidnapping occurs and is assigned to protect Franny.

Franny Perkins—Mystery writer. Lived at the Young Ranch when she first moved to Wyoming, but now lives in Hope Town. Witnesses a kidnapping when she moves to Hope Town.

Copeland Beckett—Detective with the Bent County Sheriff's Department. Engaged to Franny's cousin, Audra.

Audra Young—Rancher and Franny's cousin, who Franny has been living with up until now.

Zach Simmons—Owner of Hope Town. Married to country singer Daisy Delaney.

Brooke Daniels—Royal's sister, married to Zeke Daniels. Lives on a ranch outside Sunrise.

Lia Blair—Manages Hope Town Bakery. Franny lives in the apartment above the business.

Albennie Ward—Works at Hope Town Bakery. Franny witnesses her being kidnapped from the bakery.

Chapter One

Franny Perkins had plenty of experience being the odd one out. She was an only child who'd grown up with her nose in books, her head lost in her own imagination and no one around her quite knowing where she *fit*. Including herself.

She'd fit here, for a while. The Young Ranch in rural Wyoming. Oh, she was no rancher—she was allergic to just about every animal known to man. But she liked the mountains, the quiet landscapes. She even liked the cold—though deep in a Wyoming summer cold was a bit of a fond memory at the moment.

What she didn't like, at all, was playing third wheel. And with Copeland Beckett moved into the ranch house now that he and her cousin, Audra Young, were engaged, Franny was once again relegated to odd man out.

She'd stayed awhile. She didn't want Audra to feel bad, or think that Copeland's moving to the ranch had made her leave. Audra was the kind of person who would take the blame like that. So, Franny had taken her time, built her story, and now was putting it into action.

"It's only temporary," Franny assured Audra, even though it was a lie. "Just while I write the book. My agent was really excited about the idea of being able to sell it based on real-life experience." She'd just about finished packing everything she would need to move into the little apartment in Hope Town only a thirty-minute drive away. That was nothing. Especially around here.

Audra watched her pack her toiletry bag with mounting suspicion, but Franny kept the easy, breezy expression on her face. "It'll give you and Copeland some time to learn how to live together before I come back."

"You *are* coming back."

"Of course I am." It was a lie, and Franny hated to lie, but she'd hate it more if Audra felt guilty for a choice Franny had made. "Once the novel is finished."

By then, Copeland and Audra would likely be married, maybe even starting a family if she stretched it out long enough. If needed, Franny would create a new excuse. She would *not* horn in on her cousin's new life. Not like that.

Franny shouldered the pack of things she'd need tonight, then hefted her last box. She'd left a few things behind to give Audra the illusion that she'd be back. Some old clothes she didn't wear, a few books she'd never read again.

Audra followed her down the stairs to where Copeland was carrying the heaviest of Franny's belongings into the moving truck. He looked like he was just about done, so it was perfect timing. He'd drive her out to Hope Town in the intimidating moving truck, then go return it for her since the return center was close to his work at the police station where he had a cruiser.

It'd give Franny some time to unpack before Rosalie picked her up on her way out to the ranch so Franny could come back and get her car, eat one last dinner with her cousins while the men made themselves scarce and then make that final break—driving to her new place. Alone.

"I can ride with and help you unpack and—"

Franny turned to Audra and spoke firmly. "And you

have chores to see to. I'm thirty minutes away, Audra. Besides, I'll be back after we unload the truck to pick up my car. We'll have our girls' night dinner. You *are* making brownies, right?"

"Yes, right." Audra frowned. Her gaze drifted toward the back—where her ranch stretched out and there were indeed chores to be done and responsibilities to be met.

So Franny marched herself to the truck, put the box she'd carried in the back before Copeland brought down the door.

He walked over to where Audra now stood on the porch stairs. He murmured something to her Franny couldn't hear, then gave her a quick kiss before heading for the driver's side. Franny made sure her smile was cheerful and easy as she got into the passenger side.

Without much discussion, they started off the ranch and out to the highway. Franny wouldn't let herself wring her hands, though that's what she wanted to do. She didn't understand why she felt so damn nervous when she knew that this was what needed to be done.

New beginnings. Life steps. It was natural to feel…to *feel*. Wasn't that one of the biggest reasons she'd had to move away from her parents? She had shoved down her feelings so much so as to never worry or hurt them that she was afraid she didn't have them anymore.

Feelings were good. Feelings were her job. And her life was fairly sheltered, more or less, but less since coming to Wyoming. Life experience helped her write better books.

So this was all good. She'd never lived alone before. It was long past time she checked off that life experience.

"Thanks for the help, Copeland," she said, wanting to distract herself from her thoughts at least a little bit. Copeland wasn't much of a conversationalist, but she was desperate.

"I'm supposed to talk you out of it on the way."

"But you're not going to. Because I've already decided." She slid him a sideways glance. "And because you don't want to talk me out of it."

He sighed, looking seriously at the road as he drove. "It's a big house, Franny. There's room. I don't want you to think you're not welcome any more than Audra does."

"It's not about being welcome. It's not about…you guys." Another lie. She wrinkled her nose, trying to focus on the positives rather than her lies. "Besides, you two *lovebirds* deserve to have all that room to yourselves."

Copeland pulled a face. "Please never use that word again in my presence."

She grinned. Copeland wasn't the most affable guy—not like Rosalie's husband, Duncan. But it was obvious, no matter how prickly he was, he loved Audra *so much*, and made her *so happy*, and that was all that mattered to Franny. That her cousins, who were also her *friends*, were happy.

She didn't mind being the odd man out on that front. She was young, and sure, who wouldn't like a little romance? But she hadn't moved to the middle-of-nowhere Wyoming to find a man, even if she had the occasional fantasy about being whisked away by an upstanding taciturn cowboy.

She was here to write. To discover…who she was. She loved her parents, they were amazing, but as an only child, she'd known if she stayed in Washington, she would have lost herself in not ever hurting their feelings.

She'd needed a break, some independence. But she'd also needed some built-in friends so she didn't fully immerse herself in hermithood. Something that was far too easy for her to do.

As much as she'd enjoyed living with the Young sisters, Franny also liked being on her own. She liked solitude.

Sometimes too much. Sometimes so much her life narrowed down to nothing but fictional worlds. It wasn't good for her.

But neither was trying to constantly please people. So moving out here had been her first step toward meeting her personal goals, and now living on her own without falling into bad habits would be the next step.

It was good. It was *right*.

And she held on to that assertion as she watched Bent County pass by on her way to Hope Town.

"I'M SO PROUD of you!"

Royal Campbell stood on the porch of his sister's ranch house and grimaced as his sister squeezed him tight. He figured he owed her, more or less, though he didn't like to admit it out loud. Especially in the presence of her husband.

Zeke Daniels was an irritating SOB, but he loved Brooke, so Royal figured it gave him enough of a pass, but that didn't mean he was ever going to air any of his feelings in front of his brother-in-law.

Royal detangled himself from his sister gently. Because the whole baby bump thing she had going on freaked him out. Shouldn't she be lying down or something? But she was always moving around, that bump getting bigger every week that went by.

"Don't sound so surprised I made it off field training, Chick," he said, easing away. He was wearing a *gun* since he was in uniform and on his way into work. She shouldn't be that close.

"Why not?" Zeke muttered. Brooke gave him a little slap to the chest with no heat behind it.

"I'm not surprised at all. I am proud and happy." She beamed at him.

She deserved to be happy. And if him getting his life

together made her happy, Royal figured that was reason enough to do it.

But somewhere along the line he'd figured out he wanted to get his life together for a lot of reasons. For Brooke. To spite their father who'd been a high-level member of a horrible biker gang. And strangest of all, at least to him, was the desire to get it figured out for himself.

He'd spent his entire life reacting to the bad hand he'd been dealt. Now he wanted to turn that hand into something. Stop reacting, stop running, stop *fighting* every damn thing stacked against him and build something of his own.

"I've got to get to work. Just wanted to drop by and tell you." He took a step down from the porch so she couldn't hug him again.

"Come to dinner on your next day off."

"You're supposed to be taking it easy," Zeke reminded her. "No big meals."

"It won't be a big meal. Just an extra seat at the table." She beamed at Royal. "What day?"

Royal looked from Brooke to Zeke. He didn't relish getting in the middle of any marital arguments, but if he did, he'd be on Brooke's side. Except when it came to taking care of herself. "Thursday. I'll bring pizza."

She frowned a little, but when Zeke's arm came around her shoulders she sighed. "All right. Bring pizza."

He offered a wave then strode back to his Bent County Sheriff's Department cruiser. He got in the car, and once again reveled in having it to himself. He'd had a good field training officer, but part of why he'd applied for Bent County after the police academy had been that there was a certain amount of autonomy once you were off field training.

And now he was. He glanced at the clock. And he needed to get into the station for roll call.

It was a surprise, even to him, that he liked it. That he seemed to fit. Taking orders and following rules had never been his style. A little difficult to learn respect for authority when you grew up in a dangerous biker gang.

It wasn't *easy* to suddenly *yes, sir* everybody. It wasn't *easy* to be the rookie, knowing he got treated a little less for it, especially considering he was older than every single other rookie, and even some of the guys with a few years under their belts. More often than not, it put his back up and had those old rebellious tendencies kicking up a fuss.

But he pushed them down.

He tried to look at it as every rule followed, every pointless-feeling *yes, sir* allowed him to help someone who needed it.

And he knew the depths of needing help that some people faced. He knew the desperate lengths a person could go to in order to *help.* So any time he was tempted to tell a superior to go to hell, he remembered what he'd done in the name of justice as a boy—and how different his life might have been if there'd been someone bigger and stronger to help.

He'd be the bigger and stronger for somebody now. This time, on the right side of the law.

It still gave him a pause, now and again. The ingrained belief that the *system* was bad, and he was an idiot for falling into it. But he fought back those doubts.

Brooke was proud of him, and that held weight. He supposed he was learning to be proud of himself too.

His FTO had been pretty strict about speed limits, setting an example while in his patrol car, so Royal was careful not to speed past the slow-going truck in front of him like he wanted to. But eventually, he couldn't take it any longer, and he eased around the moving truck.

He passed, and on a sideways glance he recognized Copeland Beckett at the wheel. Beckett was a detective at Bent County, and Royal wasn't sure what to make of him yet. As a road deputy, Royal hadn't had much interaction with the detective bureau. A lot of people at the county respected the guy though, but Royal liked to make his own conclusions about people.

Case in point, the one thing he did know about Copeland Beckett was that the cute brunette in his passenger seat was *not* Copeland Beckett's fiancée.

Cops, he thought bitterly—an old habit.

He looked down at his uniform and laughed. Sometimes, life really was a kick in the pants.

Chapter Two

Franny didn't bother to unpack. She'd save that annoying chore for when she wanted something specific or when she hit a rough patch in the book and needed something to occupy her hands. Everything she absolutely required for the first few days was packed in a separate bag anyway—some clothes, toiletries, her inhaler and the like.

She did set up her workspace. She'd learned over the years that she could work anywhere, at any time, with just about any background noise, but she still liked having one organized space to go to when everything started to feel too fractured. A center.

The apartment above the Hope Town Bakery was small—one bedroom, one bathroom and then a kitchen/dining/living room area that was really just one large room. She'd had Copeland put her writing desk and office drawers up against the far wall that was dominated by three tall, narrow windows that looked out over Main Street—the only street—in Hope Town.

She took a moment to enjoy the view. Too bad she wasn't writing a historical. She could almost imagine herself as some mysterious woman from "back East," looking for a fresh start in a Wild West frontier town.

Maybe she could make the book a dual timeline. Maybe her next book should be a historical Western. Maybe…

"One book a time," she muttered to herself.

But she liked that so many ideas were already percolating. It meant she'd made the right choice.

Hope Town was an interesting place with a mysterious history. It had been a ghost town years ago, completely abandoned. Then a man named Zach Simmons, who'd been an FBI agent before he'd settled in Bent, had bought up a bunch of land and buildings and begun to revitalize the town.

The mystery was why Mr. Simmons, who owned all the land and buildings, wouldn't allow anything in that didn't meet his approval. Not a business, not a renter, no one.

Franny had needed to meet with Mr. Simmons with her rental application, answer a few questions. Provide references. He had been professional, kind, and friendly. But he'd been pretty…vague in answering her questions about Hope Town.

A little disappointing, because she wanted to get a better understanding of how the town had come to be. Not because she was writing nonfiction, just because she wanted…some framework for her idea that was based in truth and reality.

So she didn't have to get all the details right exactly as they were, but she wanted to know as much as she could. She wanted everything to feel real, authentic, and she wanted to do right by the story that had been simmering in her brain for a while now.

In her book, this town would see tragedy and fear, death and mystery, and then justice, hard won, with maybe a little romance thrown in.

On that thought, she turned away from the window, grabbed her laptop, and got to work sketching out some ideas.

Royal didn't complain about his zone assignment. Out loud. He was the rookie. He'd get the grunt work for a while yet.

A zone that included Hope Town and a handful of ranches would result in a fat lot of nothing to do. He probably wouldn't even be able to pull anyone over for a speeding ticket. If he got a call, it'd likely be for… Hell, he didn't even know out here.

One thing he'd learned about the citizens of Bent County was that a lot of them—especially the ones who lived more isolated—liked to handle their own issues. They didn't call the police for just anything.

Frustrated, he stood and moved through the room to Corporal Gardner Fairhurst, Gard to his friends—and Royal felt he'd earned the *friends* label by now. Gard had been his FTO and had been just the kind of trainer a person had to be thankful for. Calm, patient, willing to answer any question, giving solid advice, and also had given Royal the room to develop his own confidence as an officer of the law.

And since he liked and trusted Gard, Royal voiced his frustration to him, though he made sure to be quiet about it.

"Shouldn't I be put somewhere I might actually get some experience?"

"You will."

"When?"

Gard looked at Captain Kraig who still stood at the front of the room, then back at Royal. He didn't answer the question. Royal scowled in spite of himself.

"He hates me." Royal knew his past could be used against him, but he'd figured he wouldn't have been hired if the sheriff held that past against him. His record *had* been expunged. That was how he'd even gotten into the police academy, that and some of Zeke's family greasing the wheels.

But Royal hadn't considered some of the men between him and the sheriff might see it all differently.

"He doesn't trust you just yet. You'll get there. Be conscientious, ask questions or for help when you need to and for the love of God, don't complain to anyone but me." Gard clapped him on the shoulder and nudged him out of the conference room. "It'll make its way back to the captain faster than you can blink."

Royal only grunted as they made their way through the building and outside to the waiting patrol cars.

"You've got this, Campbell. *If* you can learn to swallow your tongue."

"Big if," Royal muttered.

Gard laughed. "There's always bartending," he said. "You wouldn't have to hide those tattoos then."

Royal snarled, then split off from Gard toward his patrol car. It *was* hot to be wearing this damned long-sleeved uniform, but those were the rules and somehow he'd become not just a man who had to follow pointless rules, but a man whose job it was to enforce them.

With his current zone, he had two main jobs today. Run radar on the highway outside of Hope Town, do a walk-through of Hope Town in the afternoon, and respond to any calls that came over the radio for his zone.

So, he went about his business and didn't allow himself to dwell on the fact that no calls came through for *him*, while pretty much every other deputy on the road was getting called constantly.

He'd get there, he reminded himself. Gard had said he would, and Gard hadn't steered him wrong yet.

After noon, he headed over to Hope Town, parked at the end of Main Street. The assignment here was to walk up one side of Main, then down the other. Mostly just looking for things that didn't fit in.

He'd only done this duty with Gard twice on field training, and now that Royal was handling it himself, he wondered why Hope Town got special treatment. There were other tiny map dot towns in Bent County, but this was the only one that got a Bent County daily walk-through.

Besides, what would ever "stand out" here? They had a handful of shops—a bakery, an antique store and a bookstore. There was one other building that looked like maybe it was getting a new business, but he couldn't tell what it was.

Maybe there might be some theft because of the businesses, but you'd have to be a pretty stupid thief to come all the way out here to get…what? None of these cash registers could be holding that much money.

He wouldn't complain about it though, he reminded himself. Maybe it didn't make sense, but being able to get out of the car, stretch his long legs, get some fresh air, that was definitely a positive for him.

It was eerily quiet for a sunny summer afternoon, but as he passed different storefronts, he realized that all of them that advertised their store hours said they were closed on Mondays. Still, there were people living in the apartments above the businesses, in the houses farther down the road.

It was weird to be this quiet. As he walked, he noticed up the street there was the antique store with a few cars in the lot. Somewhere a ways off a dog barked. There were signs of life here and there, he supposed.

When he came back on the opposite side of the antique store, things had cleared out again, but it wasn't quiet. He heard…swearing? He stood still, and listened to the stream of creative, threatening profanity.

Was someone in trouble? Excited for some potential action, he moved quickly toward the sounds. Behind the bakery building. He turned the corner to find a woman at the bottom of a rickety-looking set of iron stairs that led to the upper floor of the building. Maybe an apartment above the bakery.

"You okay?" he asked.

The woman stilled for a moment, before she turned toward him and blew the bangs out of her face. She looked vaguely familiar, but Royal couldn't place her. She had a bookshelf half her size leaning precariously against the wrought iron staircase.

"Just made the idiotic decision to purchase this from the antique store across the way." She gestured in the direction of the antique store. "Then thinking, oh, it's just right there, I could carry it back to my place. It's small. And it is, but it's an *antique*, so it's *heavy*. Which would have been doable, if I didn't have stairs to navigate." She sighed dramatically. Studied him for a moment, then flashed a smile. "I don't suppose you could give me a hand?"

"Not really in the job description."

"No, I don't suppose it is," she said, her gaze moving over his uniform in a way that left him…oddly uncomfortable. It was like she was filing away every button, snap, pocket and item on his belt.

"Does Hope Town have its own police dep—" She shook her head before finishing the question. "No, you're Bent County. But a deputy. How does the sheriff's department decide how to police Hope Town?"

Not quite sure where she was going with this, Royal answered the question watching the teetering bookcase and the odd—if pretty—woman. "We get assigned zones. Zone's a lot bigger than Hope Town."

"Do you get a lot of trouble here?"

He frowned at her. He wasn't used to being peppered with questions. That was usually his job. "You looking to apply?"

She laughed, the sound was surprisingly husky when she was kind of a tiny thing. "No, but I suppose the questions are a bit of a professional hazard. I'm a writer. Currently working on a story sort of based on Hope Town. Maybe. Brain is constantly in book mode at the moment."

Royal wasn't sure what to make of that. Her. This.

Before he could decide, a car pulled up and parked in the little lot behind the building.

"Oh, that'll be Rosalie," the woman said.

But Royal would have known the woman even without the name supplied. Vaguely anyway. Rosalie Kirk was a private investigator with Fools Gold Investigations out of Wilde. She harassed the detectives a lot, and occasionally the deputies if she had a case that lined up with police work.

Plus, she was married to Duncan Kirk, former professional baseball player. Pretty well-known around these parts, even if Royal had only been in these parts a few years instead of his whole life like most of them.

Rosalie walked up, carrying a big potted plant. She looked Royal up and down. "You harassing my cousin?"

"Why would I do that?"

"He's not harassing. He was asking if I needed help," the woman supplied. She smiled kindly at him. "Thank you. But I bet Rosalie and I can handle it."

He didn't point out to either one of them that he *hadn't* offered to help. Just nodded and walked away. Maybe he gave the lady a backward glance, just because she was… he didn't have the right word for it. Something about her was...*off-putting*, and he didn't know what. And he was supposed to be looking for things that felt off, wasn't he?

"I'll run up and put your *happy new place* plant inside, then come down and help," he heard Rosalie tell her.

Happy new place. New shelves. She was moving in. Rosalie's cousin.

Which was when it clicked—why she looked familiar. The moving truck.

She'd been the brunette in the truck with Copeland Beckett, though out here in the sun her hair edged toward red.

But Royal figured that was all he needed to know about her.

Even if that laugh kept coming back to him throughout the day, a haunting sound he couldn't quite get rid of.

Chapter Three

Three Weeks Later

Franny felt like she'd settled in quite well. She had a routine—one that got her out of the house most mornings for a walk, a coffee—except on Mondays, and soaking up the whole ambience of the town. Then she'd be home late morning, make some lunch and get to work…or trying to work anyway.

On Mondays, since the town businesses were mostly closed, she went to either the library in Sunrise or Bent to do some research, then swung by Audra's or Rosalie's for dinner—or they all met in town and ate out, sometimes with Vi and her kids.

Vi was Audra and Rosalie's cousin on their dad's side who lived in Bent with her husband and kids. Her husband who was a detective at Bent County with Copeland.

Those little ties always made Franny smile. Back in Washington, her life had always been so…small. They didn't have family, and while she'd had *friends*, it wasn't like her life here.

Which was good. She was feeling really positive about it…or tried to be, since she didn't have much to show for three weeks of work. She didn't usually get hung up on research when she was writing, preferring to focus on character and emotional arcs. The mystery when she got toward the end and had to figure out the bad guy, but she'd learned over the years that no book was the same and apparently this one was going to be difficult in the beginning.

That was fine. She had time.

She told herself that while lying in bed one morning, up *far* too early, but her mind turning in circles.

She'd found out so little about Hope Town, aside from its early history as a frontier town. But it's new history? Basically nothing. And when she asked a few of the residents, she'd been met with a lot of changes in subject.

Maybe that's all she needed, she told herself as she got out of bed, giving up on sleeping to a normal hour. A mysterious town. She could make up the mystery. She didn't need to discover Hope Town's.

"But I *want* to," she muttered to herself. Which wasn't a way to get things accomplished, meet her deadlines or make herself happy, but she just felt...stuck in this need to know.

Well, feeling stuck was for people who didn't have to make a living. Today she was writing that first chapter come hell or high water.

But first she needed coffee and, with any luck, a cinnamon roll the size of her face. She went to the window in her bedroom. It looked out over the parking lot behind the bakery. If Albennie's or Lia's cars were there, she'd head downstairs and beg for some before-hours service. If it was empty, she'd have to make do with the healthy food she'd been foolish enough to stock her place with, thinking living above a bakery meant she shouldn't have snacks on hand.

She glanced out the window, did a little celebratory butt shake when she saw a car in the lot, but stopped and frowned when she saw it was a big SUV.

None of the women who worked at the bakery had a big

car like that. She'd never seen a car like that...anywhere in Hope Town.

"Don't be ridiculous," she muttered to herself. Just because she'd lived here a few weeks didn't mean she knew every car, even if it was a small town without a lot of residents. She didn't care about cars. Why would she know if there were cars around like that?

Then why did it stick out? Why did it feel—

She heard something. A faint crash? Her heartbeat kicked up as she strained to hear, but she only heard the thump, thump, thump of her own pulse.

She moved closer to the window, looked down at the car. Knowing she was being ridiculous, she picked up the pen and notepad she kept on her nightstand and jotted down the license number she saw, and some details about the car.

Paranoid, paranoid, paranoid.

Before she could set down the notepad, she saw a figure. No, *two* shadowy figures come out the back door of the bakery. Muffled sounds. Sounds of distress?

It was too dark to see, but it would be easier as they moved toward the streetlight that dimly illuminated the SUV.

"This is an absolute overreaction," she told herself, out loud, but she moved closer to the window, squinting through the dark. Two figures, one much larger than the other. They were moving in kind of fits and starts.

She couldn't make out the smaller figure. It was like they had a hat or a hood completely over their head, but Franny got the impression it was a woman.

"Oh God." The smaller figure was definitely fighting back while the larger figure—a man—pulled her along.

Franny dropped the pad and pen and made a grab for her cell phone sitting on the nightstand. She cursed when she fumbled it, and it fell to the ground. She picked it back up and ran, dialing 911 as she did so.

She didn't own a gun. She didn't have a weapon, but Rosalie had left her a baseball bat by the door and Franny grabbed the bat and ran. Her exit was just the stairs to the alley, so she'd have to run down the stairs then around to the back of the building.

"911. What's your emergency?" a competent-sounding voice answered.

Franny rattled off her address as she flicked off the security system and jerked her door open. "Send the police please. Someone's being…kidnapped, I guess? Forced out of the building and she's fighting back."

"Who? Can you give me a name?"

"No, I don't know who. It's too dark, but she's fighting him." Franny made it to the bottom of the stairs. "They're in the parking lot behind the bakery, the address I gave you."

"And where are you?"

"I saw it through my apartment window. I ran downstairs—"

"Ma'am, I'm going to need you to remain inside. I'm dispatching a deputy to the address. You need to stay inside—do you understand?"

But Hope Town was so isolated. How long would it take for a deputy to get here? The woman was being dragged to the car now.

Franny looked down at her bat, the woman in her ear just a buzzing now. She clicked End on the call. She didn't want to do anything stupid, but how could she just let someone be taken against their will?

Resolutely, Franny crept forward, trying to keep her breathing even. She wouldn't run forward. She would be smart about this. She would help if she could. She'd called for help, and now she would help if she could.

At the corner of the building she could hear the scuffle. A grunt, a hushed word. But it was just…male sounding. Like the woman wasn't making any sound now.

Heart in her throat, Franny leaned forward so she could see around the corner. She saw the SUV, and a big, hulking figure all but toss the smaller figure in the back seat. It didn't seem like the woman moved.

Oh, no.

The man was in the driver's seat now. His hat had fallen off in the struggle and Franny could see him clearly in the dome light of the car. White, bald, but a short brown beard. A mark on his neck—not a tattoo, maybe a birthmark or injury? She couldn't tell from her vantage point.

She could hear sirens now, blue and red lights flashing somewhere in the distance. She looked toward the sound, willing it to hurry.

When she looked back at the SUV, it was rolling away, but the driver had looked toward the lights too.

And her.

Their gazes met. She couldn't tell the color of his eyes from this far away, but she could make out their shape—narrow, wide set.

She held her breath, frozen with fear, then demanded herself be brave. She made a step forward, lifting the bat. She'd…throw it at the windshield. She'd…

But the tires squealed into acceleration and sped off before she could do anything.

They were gone.

ROYAL WAS FIRST on the scene. He'd just gotten on duty when the call had come out. Potential kidnapping in Hope Town.

He pulled up to the parking lot behind the bakery and saw the woman from a few weeks ago standing in the glow of the parking lot light. She was in pajamas, barefoot, and held a baseball bat.

Dawn was a hint on the horizon, and nothing about the bakery or the parking lot looked particularly amiss, but he parked his patrol car and got out.

The woman rushed forward. "You have to follow them," she shouted at him. "You have to find her. They went that way."

"Who is they?"

"I don't know. I don't know. It was an SUV. She didn't want to go with him. She was fighting him. She… You have to go after them."

"We will. What kind of SUV?"

She blinked up at him, eyes lost and panicked. "I… I wrote down a description of the car, the plate. It's upstairs."

"Good. Good. Let's go." He took her gently by the arm, nudged her toward the side of the building and the stairs. Once she took the nudge, she seemed to get a hold of herself and then she rushed—jogging up the stairs two at a time, so Royal followed.

Into the apartment, through a tidy living area that included the bookcase from a few weeks ago, now full of books. She went into a room, a bedroom and straight for the bed. She bent down, picked up a notepad from the ground and then shoved it at him.

She had neat, printed handwriting. A clear description and license plate number. "This is good," he told her reassuringly. He radioed the detailed description of the SUV, the plate number so dispatch could get it sent out. Stop the car wherever it was headed.

"I—I couldn't see who it was, but if he pulled her from the bakery at this hour it had to be Albennie or Lia. They always work the morning shift. Albennie Ward and Lia Blair. Lia owns the bakery, or maybe she rents it from Mr. Simmons. I'm not sure, but she runs the bakery."

"That's all good information. Let's go back downstairs. You can show me exactly what you saw."

She led him through it. She was shaky, sometimes rambling a bit, but she recounted the crime with enough clarity Royal could see exactly how it had played out.

Gard was the second officer to come to the scene, and he helped Royal cordon off the area. Day was breaking and some of the townspeople were coming out, asking questions. Royal got relegated to keeping people out of the way. Occasionally, he caught a glimpse of his witness. She just sat, by herself, at the bottom of her staircase watching the goings-on and looking miserable.

He felt an odd wave of sympathy for her, but didn't have time to really deal with it.

When the detective showed up, Royal and Gard walked over to his car to fill him in. The fact it was Copeland Beckett had Royal remembering the moving truck. Still, he focused on the case. That was the job.

Bringing home the woman who'd been kidnapped.

"I've done a welfare check on both the names the witness gave me," Royal said to Copeland. "It seems most likely our victim is Albennie Ward. She works morning shift at the bakery. Unknown assailant, but the witness gave us a description of the suspect and the car he drove away in. Dispatch has radioed out car and descriptions. You have those?"

Copeland nodded.

"I guess you know the witness."

Copeland's gaze moved from the parking lot to Royal. "Yeah, Franny's my fiancée's cousin."

"You always help your fiancée's cousin move house?"

Copeland gave him an odd look, confusion laced with distrust. No guilt. "When my fiancée asks me to."

Which left Royal a little confused himself, like maybe he'd somehow…misjudged? Before he could determine how he felt about that, another car pulled up. Not a police vehicle, at least not marked and not one Royal recognized. He also didn't recognize the man who got out—but that gait, that grim expression. To Royal that read *all* cop.

Or worse, he determined as the man came up to them: federal agent.

Copeland cursed and Gard looked frustrated, like they both knew the guy and weren't too happy to see him. He ducked under the police tape like he'd been doing it his whole life. Maybe he was in some kind of undercover unit Royal hadn't been introduced to?

But something danced along the back of his neck, reminded him of his old life, and what it looked like when the FBI waltzed into something.

"Zach Simmons," the man said, holding out a hand to Royal, and only Royal. He didn't use the word *agent*. He didn't offer any identification, so he couldn't be FBI.

Royal took his hand and shook. "Deputy Campbell."

Zach nodded, then looked from Royal to Copeland. "Bad news. This is going to be out of your jurisdiction pretty quick."

Copeland groaned. "You didn't."

"I had to."

"Had to what?" Royal demanded.

"He's bringing in the FBI," Copeland muttered disgustedly. "Once the Feds get here, this all goes to hell."

"If it makes you feel better, it had already gone to hell," Simmons said.

Chapter Four

Franny sat at the bottom of her outside stairs and watched as the police officers did their work. She tried to focus on that—pretend like she was observing for research—rather than deal with the actual thing that had happened. The officer who wore long sleeves even in this heat drew her attention at times. She wasn't sure why. He held himself…differently than everyone else.

Sometimes she could distract herself wondering what it was. Just discomfort in this heat? Was he a secret criminal hiding behind a badge? Did he carry some horrible inner pain—watching his partner die?

But she could only distract herself with that for a few minutes at a time before the reality poked at her brain.

Albennie had been kidnapped.

Franny didn't know the woman that well. They were friendly though. Albennie had quickly learned Franny's preferred coffee order. They smiled and chatted in the mornings when Franny hung out at the bakery, but no one at the bakery encouraged…getting to know one another on any kind of deeper level. There was an odd…distance, that was unlike the stoic Wyoming rancher personality she was used to. Not natural quietness or loner characteristics. There was something far more *careful* about it.

There was something under the surface in Hope Town and Franny had a feeling she'd stumbled into the deep end—but no one wanted to tell her what that deep end was.

Frustrating, and Franny liked the frustration over the fear, so she nursed it.

She surveyed the scene. Cops everywhere. Worried people everywhere. But no answers. She'd written down that license plate, described the kidnapper, and still it had been hours with no answers.

And then some guys in suits had showed up. Franny didn't think it was her impressive imagination that the guys screamed *federal agents*. They flashed badges to the cops and looked very, very, *very* serious.

When the deputy in long sleeves pointed to her, one of the agents made their way over to where she sat.

His questions were not really all that different than any of the police officers she had talked to. She had to go through the whole thing again. Why she'd been awake. Why she'd looked out the window. Why she'd thought to write down the license plate number.

Why, why, why.

She was about to tell the agent about the driver seeing her, but he was hailed over to another part of the parking lot and excused himself.

Franny sighed and went back to observing the scene. She should probably eat or drink something, maybe get a hat or move into the shade, but she couldn't bring herself to move.

A little while later when Copeland approached, Franny tried not to grimace. She didn't want to have to answer the same questions she'd already answered *again*, even to someone she knew.

Though she had started to piece together that the federal agents had different questions for the people who really knew Albennie than the local officers had. She'd filed that away to consider later. Sitting here had allowed her to eavesdrop on quite a few questioning conversations, and she was getting a picture of two very different investigations.

"Franny."

She smiled at Copeland, then wondered why she was trying to be polite when what she really wanted to do was cry.

"We might or the Feds might have more questions for you later, but I've made sure everyone has your contact information. I haven't called Audra, but—"

Franny pushed to her feet. "I'm not going back to the ranch, Copeland."

He frowned. "Yeah, I had a feeling you'd say that. Look, a kidnapping happened right below where you live."

"It did. Are you telling anyone else in Hope Town to leave?"

He didn't say anything. He didn't have to. And before he could try a different angle, Mr. Simmons approached.

"Detective Beckett." He nodded at both of them. "Ms. Perkins. As the landlord, I just wanted to make sure that you've got everything you need."

Copeland snorted at the word *landlord*, though Franny wasn't sure why.

"I'm fine, Mr. Simmons."

He nodded. "Good. Listen, it's important for a lot of the residents of Hope Town that this…stays below the radar. Obviously we've got a police presence, and people who know Albennie are worried, myself included, but we want to keep things…safe and calm. I'm hoping you'll stay."

"Come on, Simmons. What are you playing at?" Copeland demanded.

"Not playing," he said, not even sparing Copeland a glance. "I've talked with the sheriff," Mr. Simmons said.

The sun reflected off his sunglasses, and he looked very… official even though he wasn't in a uniform and didn't carry any badge. "Hope Town will have an officer posted twenty-four-seven until the kidnapper is found. I know you're a newer tenant, and this is the kind of thing that's going to scare people off, but I'd like to extend a personal invitation for you to stay, knowing there will be extra security and precautions for Hope Town residents."

"Thank you," she said. Then smiled at Copeland. "I plan on staying."

Copeland rolled his eyes and shook his head, but he didn't offer up any compelling argument not to stay. Maybe she was a little scared, but it seemed like the safest place to be was Hope Town if there was going to be a police presence and extra security.

The deputy who'd first arrived came up to Mr. Simmons.

"Simmons. Fed wants to show you something." The deputy glanced her way, but his gaze didn't linger.

Mr. Simmons nodded. "You let me know if you need anything, Ms. Perkins."

Franny nodded, turned to Copeland. "Can I head upstairs now, Detective?" She only *kind of* said *detective* in a way that sounded dismissive—something she'd picked up from Rosalie.

Copeland scowled. "Yeah, but don't blame me if Audra and Rosalie break down your door and demand you come home. I'll come with you, Simmons," he said turning to the man. "I want to hear anything the Feds have to say to you."

Mr. Simmons didn't bristle at that, but the deputy did.

"You can't let her just go," the deputy said, looking at them all like they were crazy.

Mr. Simmons eyed him. "I've already arranged with the sheriff to ramp up Hope Town security and—"

"I don't think you guys understand. She didn't just *witness* the kidnapping." The man's gaze was dark and fierce. "The kidnapper *saw* her."

Slowly Copeland and Mr. Simmons's eyes turned to her, both with an arrested kind of concern in their expressions.

Apparently *that* hadn't made the rounds yet. Or maybe she hadn't expressly told anyone but this deputy.

"Well, hell, Franny," Copeland muttered. "That changes everything."

"SHERIFF WANTS TO see you," Gard said, grabbing Royal before he headed out of the station.

Royal raised an eyebrow but didn't mount an argument. It had been a long day out in the heat dealing with the Hope Town kidnapping and Royal was ready to go home, have a beer and maybe sit in an ice bath for the rest of the night just to get the heat of the day off him.

But the sheriff wanted to see him. "Bad see me or good see me?"

"Remains to be seen," Gard said. "But you did good today. No reason it should be bad."

Royal couldn't think of a place where he'd screwed up, and Gard's reassurance helped, but being summoned into the sheriff's office long past the sheriff's usual office hours didn't feel *promising* regardless.

Royal moved through the building, headed for the sheriff's office. In one of the waiting rooms, he spotted the kidnapping witness along with Rosalie Kirk and another redhead—he was pretty sure that was Beckett's fiancée—all sitting together talking earnestly.

He still couldn't believe she hadn't been telling everyone who questioned her about the fact that the kidnapper *saw* her. What was wrong with her anyway?

None of his business.

She looked up at him as he passed. She had a set of eyes on her—big and green, dominating a pretty, fairy-ish face. Franny Perkins. He didn't think that face quite suited the name. Then again, nothing about the woman quite added up in a sensible way, and Royal had spent most of his life making sure he sized everyone around him up with sense and reason and *reality* over emotion.

But now was not the time to ruminate on the oddity of the witness. He knocked on the sheriff's door since Miranda, the sheriff's administrative assistant, was gone for the day. At the brisk order to *come in*, Royal stepped inside.

But it wasn't just Sheriff Buckley waiting for him. It was the Simmons guy. And Copeland Beckett.

Royal didn't know what to make of any of them, or why he was here. But he didn't let that show. He nodded at his boss. "Sheriff," he greeted him. "Corporal Fairhurst said you wanted to see me."

"Deputy Campbell. You got good marks from everyone today. Handled this unique situation just as we would have wanted you to. One of those Feds said he was surprised you were a rookie. You did good."

"Thank you, sir."

"Since you've got some experience now with Hope Town, and you were the responding officer, I'm recommending you to a special assignment. Mr. Simmons here has requested extra police presence in Hope Town while the search for the missing person is going on. I'm happy to oblige, but Mr. Simmons has a…unique request."

Simmons turned to him. No one had filled him in on just what this guy's deal was, but Royal'd be damned if he wasn't some kind of Fed.

"I'd like a deputy living in Hope Town for the time

being," Simmons said. "My preference would be a female officer, but the sheriff has suggested you instead." Simmons looked him up and down. Clearly not liking the idea, but he didn't voice that. "You'll be provided an apartment above one of the empty storefronts. You'll have off time, of course, but we want someone right there, just in case something happens."

"You expecting something else to happen?"

Simmons didn't say anything for a few ticking seconds. "What we have here is a delicate situation. While the FBI work to bring Ms. Ward home, it's my job to keep Hope Town safe. We're asking for Bent County's help. And the sheriff has nominated you."

Royal looked from Simmons to the sheriff. He didn't know why this should fall on him, the rookie, but it sounded a hell of a lot more interesting than what he'd been doing. Besides, he'd taken an oath to keep things safe in Bent County. That's what he'd put on this badge to do.

"All right."

"Good. I'll get an apartment ready. Sheriff gave me your contact info. I'll text you an address in the morning with a time to meet me." Simmons turned to the sheriff. "Sheriff, I appreciate your cooperation. I'll be in touch." And with that, he strode out of the office.

Once Simmons was gone, the door closed behind him, Royal glanced at the sheriff. "What aren't you telling the Feds?"

Sheriff shook his head. "It's more what the Feds aren't telling us," he said on a sigh, nodding toward Beckett.

"There's something more to this, and Simmons is in the thick of it," Beckett said with some disgust. "I'd like to bring Franny back to the ranch, keep an eye on her myself, but… Simmons has his reasons for wanting her to stay put, and I don't think they're wrong." Beckett looked beyond frustrated. "I just wish I knew what they were."

"We've stumbled into a federal case," the sheriff said grimly. "They want our help, but they don't want us to know what it is we're helping with. We'll help, because this is our county. But I'd also like to know what they're up to and just what I'm helping with and why. Normally I would have gone along with Mr. Simmons's request for a female deputy, but you've got personal experience with federal agents."

Yeah, on the *other* side of things. The *being investigated* side of things, but Royal didn't say it out loud, even if everyone in this room probably knew. Maybe his record had been expunged, but that didn't make his past a full-on secret.

"My guess is you could sniff them out a mile away."

Yeah, the gang he'd grown up in had taught identifying Feds and cops at a glance before they'd worried about any kid being able to read. And since the sheriff was giving him that kind of credit, he figured it was worth an ask. "Simmons?"

"Former FBI, so you're not far off," Beckett confirmed. "And still neck-deep in FBI things from the looks of it since he had them on speed dial when this went down."

"I want your expertise," Sheriff Buckley said to Royal. "I want your eyes, Campbell. Normally I wouldn't give this to a rookie. These are very special circumstances. So if you don't think you can handle it, tell me now."

Royal didn't hesitate. The need to prove himself was too ingrained, even if bringing up his past made him uncomfortable. "I can handle it."

"Good. You'll still work a twelve-hour shift, focusing on Hope Town exclusively instead of the whole zone. Another deputy will handle the night shift, but you're to be on call, as well. And regardless of whether you're on duty or not, I want you watching and paying attention. Particularly to any federal agents who come around, whether they announce themselves or not."

"Yes, sir."

"Added to that, Detective Beckett has requested you keep a special eye on Ms. Perkins. The Feds didn't seem too concerned about the kidnapper coming back—another thing that makes me think there's more to this than meets the eye, but we want to ensure that no one comes sniffing around our eyewitness. And I don't just mean someone connected to the kidnapping. I want to know if the Feds are talking to her, and what they're asking."

Royal wasn't quite sure how he'd accomplish that, but he was hardly going to say he couldn't handle this. Not when it was a real assignment, and right out the gate. No, he couldn't screw this up. "All right."

"I'll expect a debrief in my email from you every night. And if you handle this well, deputy, it'll go a long way in making your rookie year a lot smoother."

"I'll handle it, Sheriff."

"Good. Go home and pack up what you need. Your Hope Town assignment starts first thing in the morning."

Chapter Five

Franny didn't sleep even though by the time she got back to her apartment she was exhausted.

She'd spent her entire evening at the sheriff's department, assuring Audra and Rosalie she was fine, listening to Copeland and the sheriff and even Mr. Simmons lay out all the reasons she wasn't in any danger.

Then repeating that to her cousins ad nauseam until they *finally* relented.

She'd showered the day off when she'd gotten back, crawled into bed and then…stared at the ceiling replaying the scene in her head, over and over again, trying to remember new details. A detail that might help.

But it was the same scene. The same feeling that if she'd been smarter or stronger she might have stepped in and *done* something about it.

Instead, the kidnapper's eyes had met hers and she had done *nothing.*

And, like both the federal agent she'd spoken to and the sheriff, she thought if the kidnapper was worried about witnesses, he would have done something about it at the time.

She considered the deputy who'd been so appalled Copeland and Mr. Simmons were going to let her go back to her apartment. He seemed to be the only one with concerns.

She rolled over onto her stomach, buried her head into her pillow. She wasn't *afraid* exactly. Not for herself anyway. She was afraid for Albennie, afraid of what this all was, but she didn't think a kidnapper who'd gotten exactly what he wanted was going to concern himself with *her.*

But she was…tense. Wound up.

"And not kidnapped so maybe stop feeling sorry for yourself," she muttered into the pillow before shoving up onto her elbows and blowing out a breath.

Okay, she wasn't going to sleep. Maybe she could work. She reached over to her nightstand where she always left her laptop and pulled it onto her lap as she sank into the covers. She didn't often let herself work in bed, because it tended to turn into a two- or three-day marathon of *sloth*, but she got to make an exception for kidnap witnessing.

She opened her book document, looked at the last paragraph she'd written…then immediately pulled up her internet browser.

She typed *Albennie Ward* into the search engine. And then spent the next thirty minutes getting more and more frustrated.

Albennie Ward didn't really seem to exist on the internet. No social media Franny could find, no public records, and that was weird considering how unique a name Albennie was. But there wasn't even the stray mention of her in the obituary of a family member or on Hope Town's bakery website.

Or anyone else for that matter.

Maybe Albennie was a nickname or a middle name, but that didn't help Franny's search any since she didn't know what her real name might be. She didn't even know how old Albennie was.

Not that finding out more about Albennie was going to

do anything. It was none of her business, and she wasn't some TV show character. She didn't think she was going to solve a crime before the FBI or the local police department.

But she was *curious*, and curiosity had led her to her career. If you asked questions, followed clues, you came up with a story.

Maybe it wouldn't be the right story, or the true story, but it felt like…something. Something better than staring at the ceiling wishing she could have been braver and stronger and *better* in a scary moment.

Maybe she could ask Lia if Albennie went by a different name, or what her background was, or if Lia had any ideas about what had happened. Except that Lia was obviously close to Albennie, and questioning Lia felt insensitive at the moment. Poking around like she thought she was a detective when Lia had no doubt already fielded tons of questions wouldn't be right.

What about Mr. Simmons? What was *his* deal?

Which lead to the next question. What was Hope Town's deal?

That was why she was here, trying to write a book, so looking into *that* was work.

She typed *Zach Simmons* into the search engine and then added FBI to the search. And a few articles showed up. Zach Simmons was a much more common name than Albennie Ward, but it was still too much of a coincidence that there was a court document from about seven years ago that included a Special Agent Zach Simmons. Something about cult members.

In Wyoming.

But he hadn't been with the other federal agents yesterday. Was he some kind of…supervisor? Was Albennie part of some… FBI thing? A cult? It would explain some weirdness.

But not the sheriff department weirdness.

Did Lia know about Mr. Simmons? It clearly wasn't a secret if it was easily searched on the internet, but had anyone in Hope Town put it together? Was Franny the only one out of the loop, or was everyone?

Franny glanced at the time on her computer. It was nearly seven now. Would the bakery open today? Would it be bustling or empty? If empty, she could maybe get some face time with Lia, but if *she* was Lia, she'd damn well be taking the day off.

She didn't think Lia was the type.

Well, there was only one way to find out. She pushed the laptop away and went to get dressed.

Sleeping be damned.

ROYAL SURVEYED THE apartment Simmons had led him into. It was above an empty storefront and across the street from the bakery and Franny Perkins's second-story apartment. If he looked out the big window in the living room, he could watch the comings and goings of both.

He could even see a little sliver of the parking lot behind the bakery building. He wouldn't be able to see the comings and goings out the back of the building, but he could see any car that came in or out of the parking lot if he was watching.

"It's a nice place. Updated," Simmons was saying. "But if you have any issues, you can call the number on the fridge. Mr. Poole handles any fix-it stuff around here. Obviously if there's something going on with the case, I'll want to know."

"Last time I checked, I report to the sheriff, not you," Royal replied without any heat.

The man didn't get offended, and also didn't offer an argument. He looked at his watch, edgier than he'd been yesterday. Not quite so cool and calm—not so *FBI*-like.

Instead, he was fidgety. Like he was waiting for something.

"Got somewhere to be, Simmons?"

He looked up at Royal. There was a moment's hesitation, then a shrug. "My wife is waiting on me downstairs. I forgot we were getting family pictures today. Felt like a normal thing to do instead of worry about Albennie. So this is a quick stop before we head into Fairmont."

Wife? Family pictures? Zach Simmons having a real life? It didn't quite compute.

But before Royal could come up with something to say to *that*, he heard the distinct sounds of footsteps on stairs. And a baby crying.

Simmons swore. "Give me a sec." He opened the front door, and on the other side of it was a woman. She had long blond hair pulled back in a clip and a screaming baby with a giant bow on her head in her arms.

She didn't look like she did on stage, but Royal recognized her immediately anyway.

"Zach, I'm losing it." She shoved the baby at Simmons, then gave Royal a pinched smile over Zach's shoulder. "Sorry to interrupt, but this one is a daddy's girl, and she's driving me insane."

Royal blinked at her once. Twice. "You're..." He didn't finish the sentence. She knew who she was.

But she did flash him a grin this time, maybe because the baby had in fact immediately quieted once she'd tucked her head into Simmons's neck.

"See?" she said, jabbing a thumb in the air toward the baby. "You do the work of carting them around in your body for nine months, shove them out and this is how they repay you."

Royal knew he shouldn't say it. He *knew* he should sound less like a moron, but something had short-circuited in his brain, probably seeing one of his favorite singers in person. "You're Daisy Delaney."

She winked at him. "In the flesh. I go by Lucy Simmons around these parts though. What's your name, Deputy?"

Daisy Delaney was asking his name, and since he was still in some kind of shock, he answered. "Royal Campbell."

"Royal. That's a cool name. I like it. And the tattoos."

"All right," Simmons said, a mixture of irritation and affection in his voice. "Let's go."

Daisy—*Lucy*—laughed, low and husky. "He's so easy to move along when I need to. Flirt with somebody and he's ready to rush me out the door."

"You're a real riot, you know?" Simmons said, nudging Daisy toward the door. "Call if you need anything, Deputy." But he had clearly already turned his attention to his family. "Where's Coop?"

"Running the streets wild," Daisy—*Lucy* said as they walked out of the apartment. "You did promise it would only take five minutes, and I *did* tell you we could postpone."

"So I take it Lia has him." Their family chatter slowly faded away and Royal stood exactly where he was in the middle of a very sparsely furnished apartment.

Daisy Delaney had said his name, complimented that and his tattoos. And weirder still, for a few seconds, Simmons had seemed very, very human.

He was married to *Daisy Delaney*. Had kids with *Daisy Delaney*.

Royal shook his head. What a weird-ass world Bent County was.

But he didn't have time to think about that too deeply. He had to get ready for work and clock in. Still, he couldn't help crossing the empty living room and looking out the big window.

Simmons was loading the baby into a minivan. Simmons had a minivan.

He shook his head. Unbelievable. He surveyed the rest of the street. Mostly empty this morning. Most of the shops didn't open until ten. Except the bakery.

He glanced at the door across the street as Simmons drove away. And thought *jackpot*, because his eyewitness was jogging down the stairs outside her building and turning toward the bakery door.

He hadn't *quite* figured out how he was going to handle keeping an eye on a virtual stranger, but he figured the first step was to not be strangers anymore.

Chapter Six

Franny wasn't so much surprised to find the bakery open as she was a little concerned for Lia not resting and taking time to worry about her friend. But as Franny stepped inside, the scents of pastry being made and coffee being brewed filled the air.

"Morning, Franny," Lia greeted her from where she was filling a pastry display with a tray of brownies. "How are you holding up?"

Franny slid her laptop bag off her shoulder and set it on one of the tables before crossing to the counter Lia stood behind. She was a tall woman with hair a little too dark for her fair complexion. It was always pulled back, and Franny had never seen her without a hairband fastened into her hair with bobby pins.

"That's my question for you this morning."

Lia smiled thinly. She wore a very simple gold chain around her neck and moved a hand up to fiddle with the little pressed flower pendant attached to it. "I'm worried, but a lot of people are looking for her. And you gave the police a ton to go on. We'd be lost if it wasn't for you, Franny. Really. There'd just be no hope."

The idea of no hope had a knot forming in Franny's

throat, but she swallowed past it. "Well, it was just…luck, I guess. If you can call anything about this situation luck."

"We'll take whatever we can get. So, you want the usual this morning, or something a little higher octane?"

"Are you sure you want to be waiting on people today, Lia?"

"Working keeps me from freaking out. So work it is. Besides, Zach asked me to stay open. Said there will be cops and Feds coming and going for a while yet. Good for business. And good for keeping me busy."

Zach. What made Lia on a first-name basis with Mr. Simmons? Just time? Something deeper?

"Yeah, I'll take my usual."

Franny waited while Lia plated up a cinnamon roll and poured her latte. Franny paid for both, but before she took them to a table and pretended to work, she couldn't help but ask…

"Lia… Did you know that Mr. Simmons was—"

The bell above the door tinkled and Lia's eyes flicked to the door, narrowed. But she smiled. "Excuse me, Franny," she said, moving back to the cash register. "Help you, Deputy?"

Franny looked over her shoulder to find the police officer from yesterday. She didn't remember his name. What had Copeland called him? It was lost in the blur of yesterday.

Franny moved to the table she'd left her laptop at and watched as Lia waited on the cop.

"I've been put on permanent Hope Town duty, so I wanted to go around to the businesses and introduce myself. Deputy Campbell." He held out a hand for Lia to shake.

She did so. And Franny watched with interest as Lia skirted a very fine line where she somehow seemed nothing but polite, but also made it abundantly clear she didn't like his profession. "Nice to meet you."

"I wasn't sure you'd be open this morning. I'm living across the way for a bit, thanks to Mr. Simmons. He said you guys have a killer coffee cake."

"Sure do. Want some coffee to go with it?"

"A large, please."

Franny watched with open curiosity. She didn't even bother to look away when the deputy flicked a glance at her while Lia got his order ready. Why shouldn't she observe?

"Here you go, Deputy. On the house."

"Oh, don't do that. I'll pay."

"It's on the house," Lia repeated firmly. Then turned away and walked into the back room, not giving him a chance to argue.

Franny heard the deputy sigh, then he turned and glanced at her. He gestured at her with his coffee cup. "Guessing you had a long night."

Franny smiled thinly. "It was certainly long."

"You were still at the station when I left." He moved over to her table, set his coffee down on it. "Royal Campbell," he offered, holding out a hand for her to shake.

Franny didn't know what to make of the fact he'd introduced himself to Lia as *deputy*, and to her he'd given his first name. A first name she immediately wanted to put in a book.

But she didn't say that, though it was on the tip of her tongue. She shook his outstretched hand and noted the tiniest hint of something dark at his uniform shirt cuff. A tattoo? Well, maybe that explained the long sleeves in this heat. He had big rough hands, a tall rangy build. Even though she didn't associate tattoos with cops, it fit something about him. That edginess she'd noted yesterday. He didn't hold himself like Copeland or any of the other cops she knew—though she supposed she was more familiar with detectives. Maybe that was the difference.

"Franny Perkins," she returned. Then wrinkled her nose. "I guess you knew that."

"I guess I did. You always work from the coffee shop?" he asked casually before taking a bite of the coffee cake.

"Uh, no. It's usually too distracting to write here. But I'm pretty sure if I stayed in my apartment today, I'd rot in bed all day."

"You probably earned it. Yesterday was a lot."

"Maybe, but if I let myself bed rot too much, I don't surface for weeks. And I can't even blame work. I won't write. I'll watch one-minute videos on how to make elaborate cakes that I, myself, will never make."

His mouth curved. He had very blue, yes, and his nose was just a shade crooked. There was a faint scar that ran down his jaw on the left side. And she should *not* be cataloguing the features of a deputy no matter how attractive he was.

"You mind?" he asked, pointing at the chair across from her.

She didn't think he was *flirting*, but she couldn't quite decide what this was. Still, she gestured at the chair as a sort of *have at*, and he settled himself in it. Every once in a while she could hear the faint sound of someone talking from his radio, or a crackle of static, but he didn't pay it any mind. He ate his coffee cake and drank his coffee.

"So, you're a writer," he said, eyeing her computer.

She nodded, dreading the next question.

"What do you write?"

It was an understandable question, and if it could just be that easy, she wouldn't mind it. But it was never just *that*.

"Mysteries," she answered, bracing herself for the next comments.

Like so and so? Have I heard of you? I don't like books with xyz in them. You can't make a living off of that, can you?

"That's cool. I guess Bent County has a lot of inspiration."

She stared at him for a full beat. Because...he didn't even say it sarcastically. "It does," she said, probably with a little too much earnest fervor, but so many people—her parents included—didn't understand why she found living here so inspiring.

"Plus you've got Beckett at your disposal, right? Probably pretty nice having a direct line to a detective."

Franny nodded. "I'm not sure if he's at my *disposal*," she said, biting back a laugh at the thought. "But he'd probably jump off a cliff if Audra told him to, so it *is* helpful."

"Audra is your...cousin?"

"Yes. You know Rosalie Kirk, right? The private investigator. Audra and Rosalie are my cousins. I lived with them for a while before I moved into Hope Town. Then *their* cousin who lived with us too is married to another detective, Thomas Hart. Do you know him?"

"Of him. I don't have much connection to the detective's bureau yet. I just started at Bent County three months ago."

That made sense. She didn't think she'd ever heard of a Royal Campbell before. "I've been in Bent County for three years now. It's kind of funny all the connections you'll make the longer you're here. But it's a great inspiration. Small towns and isolated ranches are a great setting for murder. Well, fictional murder, the real stuff is a lot less fun. I guess you'd know that."

He didn't say anything for a minute. Almost like he was

uncomfortable. And of course he was. She was sitting here talking about murder from a writer's perspective, and he saw it from a *real life* perspective. *This* was the problem with talking to people. She always put her foot in her mouth.

"Have you lived in Bent County long or did you come for the job?" she asked, trying to change the subject. She *would* have gone back to pretending to be writing, but he was just…sitting there.

"Ah… Well, I came here about two years ago. My sister… lives here. She liked it. We'd been…out of touch for a while. She's got all sorts of friends at the Sunrise Sheriff's Department and they convinced me to go to the police academy. She's done some work for Bent County, so it was an in."

"She's a police officer too?"

"No. Forensic anthropologist."

Since Franny didn't think there could be *two* of those hanging around Bent County, she leaned forward. "Brooke Daniels is your sister?"

He blinked once. "You know…Brooke?"

"Well, sort of. Let's see if I can get this right: Audra's friend's husband's brother is married to this woman whose brother is married to Brooke, and through that long line of small-town connections, I got introduced to Brooke so I could ask her some research questions. She's very nice."

"Yeah."

"And she was really helpful. She inspired a great twist for that book." More at ease with a connection to people he knew, she grinned at him. "I still owe her one."

He looked a little more uncomfortable than he had, but only for a second before he smiled. A smile she would categorize as…*rakish*, rather than polite.

Maybe he didn't *mean* it to be. Maybe that was just what happened when he smiled, but it sure did something fluttery to her chest. Which was so utterly ridiculous in this situation. What was wrong with her?

"Well, if you ever have any questions about being a rookie deputy in small-town Wyoming, you just let me know."

She nodded. Lamely. Really, really lamely.

He got up. "See you around, Franny."

"Sure."

She didn't *mean* to watch him go. It just seemed the natural thing for her eyes to follow him out of the bakery. Watch that confident stroll. She might have watched him through the storefront window until he disappeared, but Lia spoke, startling her.

"I think hot cop has a crush."

Franny bobbled, looking back at Lia—who she definitely hadn't known was paying any attention since she'd been out of sight. Now she stood at the cash register.

Hot cop. Yeah, well. "I think he's just doing his job, and I was polite," Franny said, a little stiffly. "Friendly."

Lia snorted. "If you say so."

ROYAL WASN'T SURE what had possessed him to answer so many of Franny's questions with the truth instead of easy evasions.

She knew his sister. Maybe it was as simple as that had thrown him for a loop. It shouldn't surprise him. Brooke and Zeke were part of the community. People knew them.

But he still wasn't used to how everyone in this huge county seemed to have *some* connection to each other.

He'd mostly kept to himself and Sunrise up until he went to the police academy. He knew the Hudsons and the Danielses and that was enough for any man.

His time with Bent County had opened up a new world

of people, but he still kept himself a little separate. He didn't know who knew what about who he was or what he'd done. The sheriff knew, but Royal wasn't about to advertise he'd been to jail. That he'd been framed for murder trying to save some young girls from their terrible life in the Sons of the Badlands gang.

No matter how much of a setup the murder charge had been, he *had* been a criminal, a gang member. Maybe he'd known it was wrong, but the only way he'd known how to help was from within, which meant bending some rules.

Okay, breaking a lot of rules.

And now he was on the outside, not just following rules but enforcing them.

Which meant he couldn't let an interesting woman with dreamy green eyes and an engaging smile distract him from his purpose.

Like this job. He couldn't take it for granted that it had taken a lot to get him here. He had to make sure the sheriff was pleased with his performance. Which meant, he had to find *something* to put in his report today.

So, he went into any businesses that were open, introduced himself. Down one side of the street, then up the other. Popping into the ones he'd missed once they flipped their signs to Open, chatting with any passerby.

They were not a talkative lot in Hope Town. Not that his experience with people around here meant he expected any level of gregariousness, except Franny. She was a chatter.

He smiled in spite of himself. Based on how the day was going, that had been the most positive interaction he'd had all day.

Near lunchtime, he headed for the bookstore now that it was finally open. He was almost all the way on the other end of the street, but he kept it in his sights. Noting the comings and goings.

Like the woman who walked out of the bookstore with no bags. Her outfit wasn't distinct. Just athletic pants and a T-shirt and a green baseball hat. The T-shirt was a little baggy—not out of place considering the athletic pants, but Royal studied her figure for signs of a gun.

Because she had a brisk stride. Her hair was pulled back in a tight braid. Her eyes were careful and assessing.

Fed.

Royal didn't follow her right away, but he didn't go into the bookstore to make his introductions like he'd originally planned. Instead, he kept walking down the street, glancing backward once or twice to determine where the woman was going.

When she ducked into the antique store, he took a circuitous route there himself. Luckily he hadn't introduced himself there yet, so he could step in without it seeming off or like he knew who the woman was. Or what she was anyway.

His target was talking to a woman at the cash register. It was casual, but Royal knew just from the way the woman stood that it was an interrogation—whether the lady behind the counter knew it or not.

They both glanced his way when he stepped inside. He offered a charming smile, walked right over to them. "Morning, ladies," he said cheerfully. "Sorry to interrupt. I'm just making the Hope Town rounds today."

He held his hand out to the woman behind the counter, not giving the Fed much attention, but he saw out of the corner of his eye how she edged away from the counter and headed for the door.

"Deputy Royal Campbell," he said to the woman behind

the counter. "I'm going around today and introducing myself to all the business owners."

He glanced behind him as the Fed slipped out of the front door.

Later he'd look at his body cam footage and figure out just who she was.

And what part of Albennie Ward's disappearance connected to an FBI case.

Chapter Seven

Franny chastised herself the entire time she got ready the next morning. A woman was missing, and she was doing her makeup because maybe Deputy Campbell would come back to the bakery and talk to her again?

It was gross and wrong…and it didn't stop her. She grabbed her laptop, shoved it in its bag, and then stepped out into a hot, muggy morning.

Was Albennie somewhere hot without any air-conditioning? Was she still alive? Would—

"Stop," she muttered out loud. She couldn't worry about Albennie because she couldn't *do* anything about Albennie. She had to focus on the things she could do.

Maybe Royal would have some updates. Not that she expected him to be at the bakery. He'd probably only gone yesterday as a one-off. And even if he did become a regular to get coffee to start his shift, it didn't mean they'd talk every morning.

"Because you're not going to be here every morning. This is *not* the schedule." And talking to herself out loud *outside* was not the best sign for her mental health. She made it to the bottom of the stairs and forced herself to slow down.

Just out for a casual stroll to the bakery for some food

and work. She opened the bakery door, internally chastised herself for immediately searching the room for Royal. He wasn't there, although one person was. Franny was pretty sure the woman worked at the bookstore, but she'd only talked to the manager so far. This woman was chatting with Lia while Lia worked the espresso machine.

Franny set her bag down. The door's bell tinkled, and she quickly looked behind her. She was *not* disappointed that the man who stepped inside was not Royal, because she wasn't looking for Royal.

The man got into line behind the bookstore lady. They exchanged a few words, so Franny seated herself at her table and determined she was going to write a paragraph before she ordered coffee. She opened her laptop, the book document.

Maybe she'd deal with her email first. She just couldn't think clearly if she had unread mail. Especially an email from her accountant. *Ugh.* She hated numbers and reality.

"You're working here again?"

Franny looked up and realized the two customers had left while she'd been deep into crafting a response to her accountant that wasn't: *I don't know, dude, numbers aren't my thing.*

"Just for research." Franny beamed at Lia, even though she was pretty sure the woman saw right through her.

The bell jingled, and since she was proving a *point*, she didn't look behind her. She studiously hit Send on her email. Then she stood to get in line for coffee…

Only to come face-to-face with Royal. Those eyes were so *blue.* She made a noise—even she didn't know what it was. A kind of *oof* squeak.

"Morning, Franny."

She had to swallow. Plenty of people said her name,

so she wasn't sure why in his low voice it felt…different. "Morning."

He glanced at her table. "Looks like you haven't ordered yet. Let me buy you a coffee," he said, stepping up to Lia and the counter.

"Oh, no." She followed him helplessly. "You don't have to—"

"She loves a latte," Lia said, oh *so* helpfully.

"A latte and a regular coffee then."

Franny glared at Lia, but she turned away to handle the drinks, so Franny had to smooth out her expression and smile at Royal. It didn't feel like a smile on her face. She felt awkward and like he could *definitely* tell she'd put on makeup this morning, because of *him.*

Stay inside where your weirdness belongs, Franny.

But Lia handed Royal the cups and Royal gestured to her table, so she had to walk back to it and let him put the latte mug in front of her computer, while he settled himself in the chair opposite.

She closed her laptop, since he was *staying* apparently. "Thanks for the latte. You really didn't have to."

"Community relations." He smiled at her, and she just… wasn't good at this. It *felt* like flirting, but maybe it *was* just community relations. How was she supposed to know?

Fictional people were so much easier.

"You looked like you were working hard."

"I wish. I was emailing my accountant. Which *is* hard work, because I'm trying to sound like I have any idea what he's talking about, and I most assuredly do not."

He chuckled. Which was… She didn't know. She didn't know what to do with *any* of this. Why had she *sought this out*?

His gaze tracked to the big window that looked out

over Main as he sipped his coffee. "Listen, I don't suppose you've noticed anyone out of the ordinary poking around? Maybe asking you or Lia questions?"

She held herself very still. She refused to be disappointed. Of course he was just…working a case. *Of course he was.*

But she had to clear her throat to answer. "No one's talked to me. I haven't seen anyone talk to Lia." She thought about this morning from the lens of what she should be—a careful observer in the wake of a terrifying kidnapping—instead of…whatever this whackadoodle mess was.

"There was a guy in here this morning who I don't know. But he didn't seem to ask any questions or be unduly interested in anything. He just got his coffee and left. You could ask Lia if she knew him."

Royal glanced at the counter. Lia was in the back.

"Yeah, maybe I will." But he didn't get up and do that right away.

And since this was about the *kidnapping*, and it was *professional*, she figured that meant she could get some of her own questions answered.

"Can I ask you something about the case?"

He studied her with a wariness that felt…heavier than it should, she thought. But he inclined his head in a *go ahead* move.

"It's just, I…noticed something. About the questions you guys asked and the questions the FBI asked. Where they…differed."

That wariness turned to contemplation, and then an intense concentration that did more of that heart-fluttery thing inside her chest. "Oh, yeah? How'd they differ?"

"Maybe it's because they already knew I didn't know

Albennie that well, but I heard them talking to other people and they didn't ask those people either."

"Ask what?"

"About who might want to hurt her. Ex-boyfriends or known enemies, customers who'd given a weird vibe. *You* asked people about that. Copeland too. But the Feds didn't."

He studied her, those blue eyes serious. Focused. "You sure?"

She nodded. "I started paying attention because it was just so…clear. They had a different angle. They were interested in the timing. The security cameras. More the…hows than the whys. It just made me think…" She trailed off realizing how ridiculous this was. "I'm sorry. You're a *professional*. I'm just a…bystander. You don't want to hear what I think."

"Actually I do." He leaned forward, watching her very carefully. "What did it make you think, Franny?"

Nerves danced in her chest—and they were nerves over sounding stupid and having him make fun of her, but there were also these sort of *awareness* nerves that she really didn't do well handling.

But she focused on her theory. "Well, if they weren't asking who might want to hurt her…they might already know *who*."

Royal kept *staring* at her. If she was a criminal, she was pretty sure she'd confess. Maybe even to things she hadn't done.

"They do have the description you gave, the license plate. So maybe they do know. Maybe they knew before they even got there."

Franny nodded. "Has anyone identified him yet? Found the car? Anything?"

Royal didn't answer right away. But his gaze was sharp,

attentive. She imagined he was working through a couple different problems all at the same time. Or maybe he was deciding how nice to be to the crazy writer, like he'd seen *Misery* one too many times.

"No, they haven't found anything that I know of," he finally said.

Hope folded in on itself, and she just felt unaccountably…depressed. "Maybe it never mattered I got all that information then." *Maybe you should have done something in the moment.*

"It mattered," Royal said, seriously enough she looked up from her little pity party. His gaze was blue and intense. "It will matter," he said forcefully.

And it actually made her feel a little better that he thought so.

IF THERE WAS one thing Royal hated about police work, it was reports. He'd never gone to school in any traditional sense of the word. A semester with this foster family, some homeschooling lessons with that one. Nothing in the gang, *obviously.* Well, Brooke had tried when he'd been really little. The fact he could read at all was probably thanks to her.

He'd gotten his GED. He'd passed the POST test. He'd *learned*, but writing things out was just never going to be his strong suit.

He pushed away from the table where he'd been working. If he didn't take a break, he was going to be way too tempted to hurl the computer against the wall, and since it was county issued, that probably wasn't in his best interest.

He paced the apartment for a little bit, trying to get some of the pent-up energy out of his system. He'd joined a gym in Fairmont, and he was technically off duty since it was after seven, but he didn't like the idea of being gone a couple hours even if there was a deputy on call for night shift.

Maybe he could go for a run. There wasn't a great path in Hope Town, but maybe he could carve one out. Though probably not in the dark.

He walked over to the window. Hope Town was dark and quiet below. There were a few streetlights, but beyond this Main Street everything around him out there would be pitch-black nothingness.

Royal blew out an irritated breath. Along the street on the opposite side, most of the lights in the buildings were off except for security lights in the shops on the first floor. He knew most of the apartments on the second floors were rented by the women who owned or worked in the stores.

Were there any men in this town? He'd asked Lia about the man Franny had seen at the bakery this morning and had been told Ellis Sutton was on the up and up, though he'd looked into what Lia had said just to verify.

Nothing out of the ordinary, just one of the few men with a Hope Town address.

But wasn't that in it of itself *weird*? Why did Zach Simmons only lease businesses to women? Was it some kind of…feminist outreach?

Or something more sinister.

"Not everything is sinister," he muttered to himself, mostly because he remembered that glimpse of Zach Simmons—father and husband—that had reminded Royal of the good people he'd met since moving here.

Thanks to Brooke.

Maybe Brooke knew Zach Simmons, or Zeke probably would. He could ask them what they thought.

But his mind didn't stay where it should. It flitted off.

Brooke knew Franny Perkins.

He shook his head.

"Weird-ass town," he muttered, then happened to look up to the apartment across from his. Franny Perkins's apartment.

And as if he'd conjured her, there she was in the window. In much the same position he was in—looking out at Main Street. She was illuminated by a light in her apartment. It was hard to tell from this distance, but it *felt* like she was looking over at him. He was no doubt illuminated to her too.

As if to confirm, she raised a hand in a little wave.

Not knowing what else to do, Royal raised his own hand in waved acknowledgment.

Then she turned away from the window and lowered her blinds. He watched those closed blinds for longer than he wanted to admit, wondering what a night in Franny Perkins's apartment looked like.

None of his business. But he was putting her theory in his report. Because she was on to something there. And if the Feds knew who they were looking for, it didn't make sense—to Royal's way of thinking—to keep local law enforcement out of it. What if he saw something that would connect, but missed it because he didn't have all the details?

He shook his head, closed his curtains, and went back to his report.

Chapter Eight

Franny did *not* go to the bakery the next day. She had her pride, didn't she? And since Royal had essentially caught her *window peeping* like some kind of stalker last night—even though she'd just *happened* to look over and see his lights on, and him pacing in the warm glow of them—she was staying far away from Royal Campbell.

So, she worked from bed. And by *work* she meant: updated her website, checked her social media properties, fooled around with a pitch that was *not* her book proposal, and did a quick internet search of Royal Campbell.

With only a tiny modicum of guilt about it.

She didn't find much. The social media story posted by Bent County about his hiring. He also had no social media, no internet profile.

"What is with these people?" she muttered irritably. It was like they were all…hiding from something.

Which *did* give her a little trickle of an idea for her book. What if it wasn't just *one* person hiding in Hope Town. *One* person with secrets. What if it was a town where people went to hide? And then one of the problems they were hiding from came knocking?

With the questions percolating, Franny actually pulled

up her manuscript file and put a few sentences together. Then a few more.

When her stomach rumbled, she muttered about leaving her computer. She had a first chapter, a good idea of what would happen next, and she'd even incorporated some of her research about the history of Hope Town into her fictionalized version.

She ate lunch with some malice—it was hard to eat a packet of tuna without malice. She didn't even have a bag of chips to balance out all this *health*.

Maybe she should go to the grocery store. But she could see the next scene play out in her head and she didn't want to stop and disrupt her creative flow.

A cop with secrets. A jaded FBI agent. A town inexplicably populated by people who didn't have pasts—that they'd let anyone else know about.

Since everything was clicking, after she finished eating she let herself keep writing in bed. The whole beginning took shape. Both main characters becoming real and three dimensional even if she didn't know all their secrets yet.

Who would want to? Things would get boring. Finding the answers to the questions was a journey she didn't want to end too quickly. But eventually the haze of creative clicking started to lift. Too many ideas. Too many different ways to go.

She blinked up, noted the sun was much lower in the sky than it had been. She glanced at the time. Nearly three. And she'd actually gotten some solid words in.

That called for a reward.

She had no such rewards in her kitchen, but downstairs there might be a cupcake if Lia hadn't sold out. And since she had no expectation of running into Royal at this hour, she gave herself permission to head down to the bakery.

Everything was fine as long as she didn't *change* her schedule in the hopes she might *see* someone.

Still, she didn't head down in her pajamas and hair that was still a mess of bedhead. She got dressed and brushed her hair. "No makeup. You don't usually wear makeup. Don't be that girl."

Besides, she wouldn't see him in the bakery. It was highly unlikely she'd run into him on the walk *down her stairs and around the corner.* And even if she *did*, what did she honestly think was happening here? She was a witness to a kidnapping. A woman who was *still* kidnapped. He was a cop investigating.

So.

She grabbed her purse and headed downstairs. There was only about twenty minutes to close, and there wasn't anyone inside. Lia was already clearing out the bakery case.

"I don't suppose you've got a cupcake leftover?"

Lia nodded and plated it up. She handed Franny the plate. "I think your boyfriend missed you this morning," Lia said.

Franny took the plate, trying to figure out what Lia was talking about. "Huh?" Confusion gave way to realization at the teasing glint in Lia's eye. "Oh, don't be ridiculous."

Lia shrugged. "He asked about you."

The little flutter she was trying to quelch did the opposite of quelch. "He did?" Before Lia could confirm, Franny waved it away in irritation with herself. "Oh, who cares. It's not high school."

"Have a lot of hot cops interested in you in high school, Franny?"

"I didn't even have ugly criminals interested in me in high school, Lia." Which made Lia laugh and Franny smile in spite of herself.

"Well, he had some news on the case," Lia said, busying

herself with cleaning out the baked goods case, but Franny could see the nervous energy in it. "I guess they found the kidnapper's car, but it was abandoned. However, they're hopeful that there didn't seem to be any signs of blood or struggle. It was in Idaho, so the Feds will start focusing their attention there."

"Idaho," Franny echoed. Albennie had been taken across state lines—which explained federal involvement, she supposed. But hadn't they been involved before they knew that? Or had they known that before?

"But you know…" Lia stopped what she was doing, looked at Franny over the bakery case. "Deputy Campbell comes in here and tells me the Feds are gone, then a little while later, this lady comes in. Pretends it's casual, but it felt…purposeful. I'd have pegged her for a cop, but she's not Bent County. I'm not sure what she is."

"Did you tell Royal?"

"First-name basis now?" Lia asked, still teasing, but she must have noticed Franny's discomfort with it. Because here they were talking about Idaho and abandoned cars and still no signs of *Albennie*, and Franny didn't think *laughing* or *rolling her eyes* about Royal was the right thing to do in this moment.

Lia sighed. "Look, I've…been through my share of stuff. Danger and worry, growing up. You learn to…accept what is. Shove down all the fear, and if you deal in a little humor to distract yourself then, well, I don't know if it's healthy or not, but it works."

Franny nodded, but she couldn't quite buy in. Not right now. "I think you should tell him."

Lia bit her bottom lip. "I was thinking about telling Zach."

"You…trust Mr. Simmons?"

Lia eyed her in that way that was becoming very common. Like everyone knew what was going on but her. "I do," Lia said after a while, but she was very serious about it.

"Then maybe you should tell both of them."

Lia nodded slowly. "Yeah, you're right. Can't hurt. What can hurt?"

For a moment, just a flash, Franny saw a kind of fear and desperation in Lia's expression that Franny had never seen there before. But quickly, Lia blinked it away.

"I'll tell Deputy Campbell about the lady next time I see him. And Zach. Hell, I'll tell the sheriff if I see him. Whatever might help. But listen, I get through each day with the knowledge that Albennie's tough. She's had to be. She's going to get through this. I have faith."

But Franny knew what it sounded like when you were trying to convince yourself of something that wasn't necessarily true. Still, she wasn't about to disagree. "Me too."

ROYAL DIDN'T ALLOW himself to develop a routine, and this morning at the bakery had been a good reminder he shouldn't.

He still didn't know what had possessed him to ask the bakery manager about Franny. Why should it matter if Franny Perkins was there or not? It didn't. He was just observing.

So after grabbing his coffee, instead of doing a walking route around the town, he got in his cruiser and took a drive around the outskirts of Hope Town. He still hadn't figured out if the woman who'd been walking around yesterday was a Fed, and he didn't know what kind of car she was driving, but he kept an eye out.

If the Feds were gone, she probably wasn't here anymore, but he wanted to be sure. And he couldn't help but think about Franny's point yesterday. The Feds hadn't asked about Albennie's past.

Not that it mattered. Everyone he'd questioned that morning had basically said they didn't *know* about Albennie Ward's past. Not where she'd moved to Hope Town from, if she had family nearby or not. They'd never seen family or a boyfriend. She was a woman who'd appeared one day and mostly kept to herself.

He thought *maybe* Lia Blair knew more and wasn't saying, along with the bookstore owner he'd talked to, but he kind of wondered if they were just keeping their friend's secrets—not trying to impede an investigation. He kept expecting the sheriff to pull him. There was a time clock ticking on this—and since the Feds had announced they'd found the getaway car in *Idaho*, Royal just didn't see how much longer Sheriff Buckley could justify him being here.

Royal kept chewing over that story from the Feds. It struck him as all wrong. If a guy was going to leave a car behind—he sure as hell wouldn't leave it anywhere near where he was headed.

Royal should know. He'd left a few cars behind in his day.

After a morning of driving around and seeing a fat lot of nothing except what he always saw, he parked behind his building and got out for his foot patrol. Nothing, nothing and more nothing. Not even the odd stranger.

But the business owners he'd introduced himself to the first day tended to wave or nod or greet him. Sometimes they introduced him to one of their staff. He was considering going to the bookstore and seeing if they had any of Franny's books. What would be the harm in reading one, getting a sense of what she did?

But he heard his voice being called before he could make a move to walk toward the bookstore.

He glanced over his shoulder to find the woman who was dominating way too much of his thoughts lately—considering he was on special assignment and he barely *knew* her.

But she bustled across the street and up the sidewalk. He met her halfway. She didn't look upset but determined. "Everything okay?"

"As okay as it can be, I guess. Are you busy? Can you come over to the bakery?" she asked, those pretty eyes intense and direct. They looked greener outside. Something about the lighting, he supposed.

And since that was *not* what he should be thinking about, he squinted across the street. "Isn't it closed?"

"Lia's closing up now, but she wanted to tell you something. She was going to do it tomorrow, but I happened to see you, so I thought I'd just act as middleman."

"All right." He followed her down the sidewalk and across the street. She knocked on the bakery door that was now locked, but Lia came right over and opened it up for them.

"I thought you could tell Ro—Deputy Campbell about that woman now, since he was right there when I walked out."

Lia looked from Franny to him. "Yeah. Sure." She wiped her hands on the towel stuck into the tied belt of her apron and held the door open for them to step inside. She didn't look *nervous* exactly, but definitely unsure. "It could be nothing."

"Which means it could also be something," he replied. "Being a cop involves all sorts of somethings and nothings."

She smiled thinly. "I've always hated cops."

"Hey, me too."

He clearly surprised a laugh out of her, and a curious look from Franny, but he listened to Lia talk about a woman who'd come in asking questions that didn't sit right with her.

He thought of the woman he'd seen yesterday. Popping into businesses. Talking to the clerk at the antique shop. He still didn't have an ID on her. "Describe her for me."

Lia's description was dead-on to the woman he was thinking of. He frowned. The rundown sheriff had given him this morning had said the Feds had left for the time being.

But if *she* was here this morning, had they? Were they lying about this too? Or were his instincts off and she wasn't a Fed at all? Did that make *her* a sinister addition to this town?

Two pairs of female eyes studied him, clearly waiting for him to do something with the information. He could keep it to himself. Keep them out of this.

But people came and went from Lia's bakery all day long. And Franny was a witness in the kidnapping. It seemed the more they knew, the better they might be able to help.

"I saw her yesterday poking around. I think she's a Fed."

"But you told me this morning the Feds had moved out."

"That's because I'd been told they had. And maybe she did after she got one more look at the scene of the crime." But it didn't sit right. Like *maybe* he'd been told something that wasn't true at all.

"I'm going to tell Zach," Lia said.

Royal tried not to bristle. "What's Simmons going to do?"

"He used to be FBI," Franny murmured, clearly considering this new information more than what she was saying.

She lifted her gaze, noted Lia and him staring at her. She shrugged. "I did an internet search. It's no secret."

Royal had been so distracted by the case—and maybe Simmons being married to Daisy Delaney—he hadn't looked into him any deeper than making note of what all he owned in Hope Town and how long he had.

"Who else did you internet search?" Lia asked.

An interesting shade of pink crept into Franny's cheeks. "Look. Isn't it clear the Feds and the sheriff's department aren't sharing information? Why would that be?"

"I don't know," Royal said irritably. He knew the sheriff didn't know either.

"It's why you're here, isn't it?" Lia said, nodding her chin across the way. "Why Zach let you lease that place."

He eyed her, wondering how much she knew. How much Simmons knew. It didn't matter, he supposed. The point was to pay attention to the Feds.

"Listen, if either of you see her again, you give me a call. A text. Let me give you my cell number." He rattled it off for them as they put it in their phones. "I don't care if I'm on duty or not. You see her, you let me know ASAP."

They both agreed.

So he moved for the door, held it open for Franny who stepped out with him. Lia locked the door behind them.

For a moment, Franny didn't start walking for her apartment and he didn't start working to continue his foot patrol.

He glanced down at her. He knew he should just say goodbye and move on with his day. But he couldn't quite resist… "Did you internet search me, Franny?"

She stared at him a full beat, her cheeks getting pink again. Then she shrugged. "For a unique name, there isn't a whole lot about you online."

He grinned, couldn't help it. There was just something about a woman who doubled down.

"And just so we're clear, I wasn't spying on you last night." She said this *very* formally as the blush on her cheeks just deepened.

He could not figure out for the life of him why she entertained the hell out of him. "I didn't say you were."

"I just happened to look up and…there you were."

"Same."

"Okay. So. Okay." She took a step away, then turned around to walk away. He could only categorize what she was doing as a *scurry.*

Which for some reason had him opening his mouth when he should keep it shut. "You know, you owe me a cup of coffee."

She stopped, turned. "I…do?"

"Sure. I bought you one yesterday, now it's your turn."

She opened her mouth, shut it, drew her bottom lip through her teeth—which wasn't fair considering he was on duty and had to keep *some* semblance of his attention on work not…her.

"I… I'll be at the bakery in the morning then," she said. She smiled.

So he smiled back. "Good."

Chapter Nine

Franny had a bit of a struggle getting into the swing of things once she got back to her apartment.

If she was back at the ranch, she'd be dissecting that moment outside the bakery with Royal second by second with Audra and Rosalie. Except Rosalie didn't live at the ranch anymore and Audra would be cozied up to Copeland where she belonged.

So Franny only had herself to go over that moment outside the bakery. He'd been flirting with her. She was *almost certain* he'd been flirting.

Right?

Then he'd asked her…to buy him a coffee. Which wasn't a date. He would be *on duty.* It was just…

Oh, she didn't know.

And since she didn't know—what to do about Royal, Albennie, Feds and cops alike, she figured she'd focus in on the one thing she *did* know.

Her book. So she made herself a decently healthy dinner, then settled down at her *desk* like a grown-up, and got to work.

And work she did. The words were flowing. She didn't even pay attention to the time. She wanted to ride this wave of everything making *sense.* And being within her control. No outside world allowed to invade.

But eventually…the words petered out, and she was yawning more than she was getting words down. She noted the time—well after midnight. The entire room around her was dark except for the light of her computer. Man, she hadn't been that in the zone in a while. It felt *good.*

But if she was going to get up early enough to meet Royal for coffee, she was actually going to need to set an alarm. And she needed to get *some* sleep so she didn't look like a total zombie in the morning.

Not that it mattered if she did or not, since it wasn't a date. He was working a case. The end.

She picked up her phone and started to head to the kitchen to get a drink of water, but that's about when she noted the odd noise.

It sounded like…scratching? At the door? She frowned. Had someone's cat gotten loose and was trying to get in?

You might as well throw a grenade in her apartment as allergic as she was to cats. Did she even know where her antihistamine was? She did have an inhaler in the bathroom, and one in her purse, so that was good.

And she wasn't going to let a cat in anyway, so what was she worrying about? She shook her head.

But something was *definitely* scratching at her door.

Just a cat, she assured herself, but… Why would a cat climb the stairs and scratch at her door? She crept closer to the door, put her eye to the peephole.

She couldn't see anything. *Probably because it's dark, Franny.* But usually there was a little hint of the security light over by the antique store when she looked through the peephole at night.

Maybe it was out. She almost never looked out the peephole, so maybe she'd been imagining a light before. Thinking it was anything sinister was overreacting.

Except a woman was kidnapped from this exact place just a few days ago.

Still… She looked down at her phone. 911 was over-the-top for some *scratching at her door* when she couldn't tell what it was. And she wasn't about to open the door and find out.

Maybe there was some sort of nonemergency line at the sheriff's department she could call. Ask for…advice? Or…

She opened the contact and pulled up Royal's number. She could just text him. Or even call him and just ask him to glance over at her place from his window and see what was making that noise at her door.

She'd almost talked herself out of it when the doorknob seemed to…creak, like it had moved…ever so slightly.

Her heart leaped into her throat, and she backpedaled into her room—closing the door and locking it too. She leaned against the door, fear making her feel numb. She managed to hit Call on Royal's number.

It rang four times and she was about to hang up and call 911, embarrassment be damned, when a rough, sleepy voice answered.

"'lo."

She'd clearly woken him up and felt like a complete ass. "Hi, sorry. It's late. Sorry."

There was a beat of silence, then two. "Franny?" he asked, like he wasn't quite sure.

And why would he be sure? She'd woken him up. It was the middle of the damn night. "Yeah, I'm sorry. I'm sorry. It's just, I think… I think someone is like…at my door, or something." Her heart was beating triple time, and she could hardly hear him over the sound of it so loud in her ears.

"What?"

"I almost called 911, but I'm not sure. It could be a cat. A dog. The wind? But it just...won't stop and I thought well... I have your number and you can look over and see. And if no one is there, I can just...curl up in a ball and only be embarrassed in front of you."

She heard the sound of rustling and movement. "Someone is trying to break into your place?"

"No. I don't know. There's just this noise at my door, and then the knob kind of moved and... Everything is locked and—"

"It's too dark." His voice was firm and with it now, no sleepy notes to it. "I can't see anything. Look, I'm going to have to hang up, but you stay where you are. I'm coming over."

"Oh, don't—"

But the connection ended. And even though she felt silly for calling him over, she was *relieved* he was coming and taking her paranoia seriously.

She really wanted it to be paranoia.

ROYAL GRABBED HIS GUN, shoved his feet into the unlaced boots by his door and ran down the stairs to the street.

Before he'd even crossed the street to Franny's side, he heard the rumble of an engine getting farther and farther away. No lights anywhere, but if someone *had* been trying to get into Franny's apartment, they likely would have kept their car lights off.

Cursing, he sent a text to the night shift deputy asking him to be on the lookout for a car driving around without its lights on. Gun in hand, he moved swiftly and silently to Franny's stairs. It was dark, but he didn't see so much as a shadow or hear anything either.

Figuring a knock would unnecessarily scare her, he sent her a text to let him in the door.

It took a few seconds, but eventually she did. She was still dressed in the shorts and T-shirt she'd been wearing at the bakery this afternoon.

"No one here," he said. He didn't have his holster on, so he couldn't put the gun away. He could see her worried gaze on it, but there was nothing he could do in the moment.

"No one," she echoed looking into the night around them. "I'm just…being paranoid. I'm so—"

Before she could apologize again, he steamrolled over her. "I don't think so. I heard an engine. Already on their way out of town when I got out. But there's not usually much going on this time of night. Doesn't feel like a coincidence. I texted our night shift guy and he's on the lookout. We'll see if he comes up with anything."

"So someone was really…"

He could hear her panic, so he thought it best to give her something concrete to do. "You got a flashlight? I left mine back at my place."

"Just my phone."

"That'll do for now. Give me some light on the outside of the door."

She did as she was told, training the light on the outside knob. Royal didn't touch the door, but he studied it. There were some scratches around the keyhole but that could have been from anything—including Franny herself not always getting the key in the first time.

He looked around at the little landing outside her door. "Anything look out of the ordinary?"

She took her time, shining the flashlight on different things. The light bobbled a little bit, but she was mostly keeping it together.

He saw it before she did, a little piece of paper tucked under her cheerful doormat. The light left the corner, but before he could ask her to bring it back, she did, focusing the beam on that piece of paper.

"That… I don't think that was there," she said.

"I don't suppose you've got any rubber gloves?"

"Uh, no."

"All right. Close the door. *Lock* the door. I'm going to go grab what I need. I'll text you when to let me back in, okay?"

She looked around helplessly, and Royal didn't know what else to do except give her arm a little squeeze, a little centering. "It's going to be okay. Just follow my instructions, all right?"

She nodded.

He stepped back from the door and waited for her to close it. She did, and he waited to hear the lock click.

Once it did, he jogged down the stairs, nearly tripping over his untied laces halfway down. Cursing himself but not wanting to stop and bother with tying them, he hurried back to his place.

He needed some stuff from his gun belt. And to put some real clothes on. The athletic shorts and unlaced boots combo wasn't exactly a professional look, but he was hardly going to put on his full clown outfit in the middle of the night.

It was too hot for a hoodie, so he grabbed the first T-shirt his hand landed on and pulled it on. Found some socks and put them on awkwardly as he went to his belt and grabbed it. Rather than fasten it around his waist he just carried it, shoving his gun into the holster.

He jogged back across the street, this time having the

presence of mind to lock his own apartment up first, then he kept an eye out for movement or sound.

Nothing. With his free hand, he pulled his phone out of his pocket when it dinged. It was a text from the night shift deputy that he read as he climbed Franny's stairs again.

Haven't seen a soul.

Royal inwardly cursed, then pulled up his messages with Franny and told her to open the door.

She did so right away, light from her apartment spilling out. He handed her his gun belt. "Hold that."

"It's heavy," she muttered when she nearly dropped it. But he ignored her. He'd already gotten the gloves out of the belt. He pulled them on, then picked up the piece of paper.

It was actually more like an index card. Folded in half. Royal unfolded it. The print on the card looked like it was from a typewriter. He frowned at the odd conglomeration of codes and words.

There were some numbers and letters in the upper left-hand corner that didn't make any sense. Then: *Perkins, F.M.* Underneath it was the phrase *Dead in the River.* Before he could read the rest, Franny spoke.

"It's a card catalogue card."

"What's that?"

"They used to have them in libraries so people could find books and where they were shelved." Her voice was weird. Kind of flat. "That one's for my first book. *Dead in the River.* It's my book."

"Oh, so it's yours? You just dropped it?" He held it out to her.

She shook her head, refused to take it. "I only even know what a card catalogue is because I took a library class in college. I've certainly never seen one for my books. They don't really use them anymore. They're obsolete."

"So... This card for your book isn't yours, but it's somehow under your doormat? After you heard someone messing with your door? In the middle of the night?"

She audibly swallowed, looking up at him with big green eyes. Fear the predominate emotion there. She nodded.

It wasn't a threat *exactly*, but it sure felt like one. "We're going to have to go into the station."

Chapter Ten

Franny sat in the passenger side of Royal's police cruiser, her nerves strung tight. She clasped her hands together and looked straight ahead.

She didn't know what to think. She did know it was… terrifying. Because she couldn't think of any good reason that card should be sitting on her porch. No, not sitting. Tucked under the doormat—but visible enough she would have seen it in the morning. Picked it up and opened it.

Her imagination went in about fifty different directions.

Every single one of them bad.

But the police would handle it. Royal would handle it. He'd come over and handled it when she'd called. It was relief and comfort and some semblance of security all wrapped into one thing keeping her anchored rather than in a full-blown panic.

When he'd first shown up, he'd been wearing what he'd clearly slept it. Low-slung athletic shorts and not much else.

He didn't just have *a* tattoo on his arm, he had a *plethora* of tattoos over the upper half of his body. Black-and-white and full-blown color. All down both arms, and on parts of his chest and back. And he was *built*, which was a ridiculous thing to think about, but it felt safer than her imagination taking her down the road of: *someone is out to get you.*

"You have a lot of tattoos." What a truly ridiculous thing to say. "Sorry, I'm tired. I say weird things when I'm tired." Sure, that's what it was.

"I do have a lot of tattoos," he agreed, sounding so calm. But he hadn't been calm before. Not deep down. He had a… professional *restraint* she supposed, but she'd seen something in his expression back on her porch that if she put in a book, she'd describe as lethal.

She really didn't want anything to be lethal right now. Even concerning him.

"No tattoos for you, Franny?"

She shook her head, gripping her hands tighter. Trying not to think about *lethal things*, and knowing he was trying to keep her distracted. "No, I'm pretty straight and narrow and boring."

His mouth curved ever so slightly. "We're riding to the police station in the middle of the night in my cruiser. I don't think you're boring."

She laughed, though it bordered on hysteria. No this wasn't boring. It was terrible. But she was just overreacting. If she breathed, thought it through, this was just a bunch of odd coincidences.

It had to be.

"So, look, I can't help but speculate. Occupational hazard." Because she needed this to be her imagination and nothing else. "So please tell me I'm just a writer out of touch with reality. Because what it feels like is someone involved with the kidnapping figured out who I was, found or made that card, then left it on my porch in a threatening manner—during or after trying to break into my apartment." She looked over at Royal.

His gaze flicked to her then back to the road. He said nothing.

Which did *not* help the tightening anxiety in her chest. "Tell me that's far-fetched," she demanded, knowing she sounded a little panicked.

"Okay, it's far-fetched."

"Royal."

"Do you want the truth, or do you want me to say what you want to hear?"

"I want the truth, and I want the truth to be what I want to hear."

He pulled into the parking lot of the Bent County Sheriff's Department, parked the car and then looked at her.

"I know you're scared. You've every right to be." His tone was firm and reassuring. He knew what he was doing and everything was going to be okay.

She could almost believe it.

"That's why we're going to go into the station, talk to the sheriff, and maybe Detective Beckett, and decide what to do to make sure you're safe."

She squeezed her eyes shut, any calm she'd managed to grab onto evaporating. "Oh, no, don't call Copeland."

"Why not?"

"Because he'll tell Audra. Audra will tell Rosalie. And together they'll worry and fuss and *worry*."

"Okay, I'll tell him not to tell Audra."

Franny shook her head. "He won't be able to lie to Audra."

"All the cops I know are great at lying."

"Sure. But not to the fiancée they love. Hopefully."

His expression was dubious, but she didn't want to argue about this. She wanted… Oh, God, she didn't know.

"Come on." He got out of the car, and she had no choice but to follow. He led her into the station. It wasn't bustling exactly, but there were more people and more things going on than Franny might have expected for this time of night.

Phones ringing. People talking in low murmured voices.

Royal led her into a room that looked like some kind of break room. "Sit here. Help yourself to some coffee or water or whatever you can scrounge up in the fridge. I'm going to go handle the evidence and make those phone calls and I'll be right back, okay?"

She nodded, not knowing what else to do. This felt like an utter disaster. So she sat at the table. The room was cold, the chair was cold. Everything felt cold and…out of body.

But Royal crouched down in front of her. "Franny."

She stared at him. His face was becoming familiar, which was strange. She'd had coffee with him twice. Talked to him in the street once, well twice if she counted him responding to Albennie's kidnapping. No…three times. She'd seen him in passing the first day she'd moved in. Still, it wasn't enough to be comforted by someone's presence.

Except he was a serious, capable police officer. He'd helped her, multiple times. She was in good hands. Everything would be okay, because what other option was there?

Kidnapping. Gruesome murder. Etcetera.

"Franny," he said again, more sharply this time, like he understood her panic was driving the brain bus. "The important thing is, even if this was a threat, nothing happened. They didn't break in, if that's what they were after. You called me, just like you should have, and now we've got evidence and another step to take. But most importantly, Franny, you're safe."

She swallowed at the lump in her throat. It didn't go away. The fear didn't go away. But it steadied. Because if he could look her in the eye and tell her she was safe, she could almost believe it.

THE FIRST THING Royal did was scrounge up something to keep Franny warm. The AC in the building ran high in these hot days of summer even when the nights cooled off. She had to be freezing in her shorts and T-shirt. He hadn't been issued a jacket yet since it was summer, but Vicki at the front desk had an extra sweater and let him borrow it. He brought it to Franny and she thanked him, still looking lost and afraid.

But she didn't cry. She didn't demand to leave. She didn't break down. She just sat there, waiting.

It made him…uncomfortable in ways he didn't understand. Pretty much everyone he'd known before the age of twenty-one had been through ten times worse than a little kidnap witnessing and subsequent break-in attempt, so why should he feel sorry for her?

But he did.

Still, he focused on what had to be done. He called Copeland, got cussed out for the courtesy. Still, the detective was on his way. So was the sheriff. He got the card logged into evidence.

Royal didn't let himself worry about Franny. She was holding up. He knew looks could be deceiving, but she just seemed…soft. Not jaded or traumatized by life. And still, she was holding up.

He didn't know why he felt *proud* about that. Had nothing to do with him.

Once he'd done everything that needed to be done before anyone else arrived, he went back to the break room to find her. He assumed they'd move to the sheriff's office to discuss what had happened, but not until the sheriff got here.

She sat at one of the tables, chin resting on her hand. She was doing something on her phone, but every few seconds her eyes would droop, close, then she would blink them open and straighten.

She didn't look up. So he found himself just standing there…studying her. The harsh lights made her hair look lighter, almost red, and her skin paler. Or maybe that was the exhaustion. She just seemed…delicate. Not *fragile*. She was dealing with some stuff and she didn't break, but there was just something…*something* about her he couldn't articulate to himself.

And probably shouldn't.

"Campbell."

Royal looked behind him to where his name had been called. Detective Beckett was striding up the hall. Behind him was a pretty woman that Royal knew was the detective's fiancée. Franny's cousin. Audra.

Royal straightened, glanced back at Franny. She must have heard his name too, because she was staring at him now. Did he know he'd been watching her?

He shook his head. Didn't matter. He pointed into the room. "She's in here," he told Beckett.

Franny stood as Copeland and Audra entered the room. Her expression fell.

"Oh, Copeland. I wish you wouldn't have brought her."

"I know," the detective replied.

"I'm taking you back to the ranch," Audra said, crossing to Franny, putting an arm around her shoulders like she was going to march her right out of there. "Right now."

"I'm afraid that's going to need to wait," Royal interrupted. "We've got a lot to figure out before Ms. Perkins can leave."

Audra scowled at him, but thankfully the sheriff arrived. "Beckett. Campbell. My office." He moved on without saying anything else.

Beckett moved over to his fiancée, put his hand on her back, the touch intimate. "Take her into the detectives' office. It's more private."

Weird, weird, weird to see people who only existed in the context of work just be…real people. But Audra nodded and pulled Franny up from her chair and before they could exit the room, Royal stepped out.

Beckett led the way to the sheriff's office. Royal knew he should just follow, but he couldn't resist a glimpse back at Franny and Audra heading the opposite direction. Their gazes met for about one second before Audra dragged Franny around the corner.

When Royal forced himself to move forward, Beckett was looking at him, but Royal ignored the study.

The sheriff was already sitting behind his desk when they entered his office. It was the middle of the night, so Royal didn't hesitate. He laid it all out for the sheriff.

The potential break-in. The catalogue card now in evidence. *And* how he considered it a purposeful threat against the eyewitness to the kidnapping.

"It doesn't seem like a coincidence we get word the Feds are pulling out this morning, and this happens tonight," Sheriff Buckley said, tapping his fingers on his desk.

"No, it doesn't," Royal agreed.

"We'll have the card processed, see if we can get some prints, but if it was left there on purpose as a threat, it'll be clean," Beckett said.

Royal agreed with that too. "I'll talk to Deputy Mayfield once I'm back in Hope Town. He didn't see anything specific, but maybe there was something of note earlier in the night. Or an idea of where they would have gone to avoid him. I *heard* a car. Maybe security picked something up.

I'll contact Simmons in the morning too, see if we can't get a look at some video."

The sheriff nodded. "Good first steps. But before we can do any of that, we have to deal with what we're going to do about our victim slash witness."

"She can't go back to that apartment if she's being threatened," Beckett said.

"But if she's being threatened, she can't just go *anywhere*," Royal returned. "She has to be protected."

Before the sheriff could weigh in, Zach Simmons strode into the office. He looked a little worse for wear. He had dark marks under his eyes and his hair was wild—probably from raking his fingers through it. He did not give off the same *I've got this* aura he always had before.

"What are you doing here, Simmons?" the sheriff asked irritably.

"I need to be part of the discussion about this attempted break-in."

"How'd you find out about it?" Beckett demanded. "It's the middle of the damned night."

Simmons shook his head. "Listen. This is more delicate than you guys understand."

"So, enlighten us," the sheriff replied. "Now."

Simmons looked around the room, surveying each of the men. "Okay, but it has to stay in this room. What I'm about to explain is private, privileged information and I am only sharing it to keep everyone involved as safe as possible. It cannot go out to the department at large, or people you all may know personally. You've all taken oaths to uphold the law to *help* victims—so I need you to understand that if what I tell you goes beyond this office, you are breaking that oath."

Royal had *felt* like there was something strange about

Hope Town, but this was more than strange. Especially when Simmons waited for every man to verbally agree.

"Hope Town is…complicated," he said, raking a hand through his hair. "And there are a lot of reasons I don't tell most people about that complicated background. That's the whole point of Hope Town. Not knowing."

He looked at each of them, as if taking time to make eye contact so they'd all understand the gravity of the situation.

"It's a place for…people who are in danger to go to live a normal, *safe* life."

"So WITSEC?"

"More like…private WITSEC, with a few more complications and a little less red tape." Simmons shrugged. "Not all of these women would qualify for a federal program, and not *everyone* in Hope Town needs protection, but there are a group of women who do, who have pasts. Ones that could catch up with them if I'm not careful. And I've been incredibly careful. I realize this attempted break-in is a concern. It is for me too, but it can't get out. It can't… These women need to know they're safe."

"But one of them wasn't," Beckett pointed out.

"No. Albennie wasn't. That's part of the problem. There was a leak somewhere. Maybe it was Albennie herself. But until I know for sure, I need to keep everyone in one place. Protected. But more, so I can get to the bottom of how who took her found out where she was. The Feds are aware of Albennie's past, and they're working from that angle, but so far, they haven't gotten anywhere."

"We're handling the attempted break-in, Simmons," the sheriff said firmly. "I trust my men better than any FBI agent. We'll share what we find, but it's our case."

"Look, I don't care who does what as long as we're all on the same page. I cannot afford for any of the women in

Hope Town to think they're not safe—or even more *not safe* than they usually are. It leaves too many of them open for their pasts to come back and haunt them. This break-in attempt *has* to be kept on the down-low."

"What exactly are you asking us to do?"

"Investigate. By all means. I'm not standing in the way of that, but I need Ms. Perkins to stay put. Her leaving would worry too many of the women and have them contemplating the same."

"You can't be serious," Beckett said.

"If this kidnapping has made Ms. Perkins a target? We need to use her."

"Mr. Simmons, I don't know about all that," the sheriff said. "She's a civilian. Not one of these other women with pasts."

"Yes, that's the point. *Normal* life. Not just people like them, but regular people too. If Franny runs at the first sign of danger, how do I keep anyone else calm and staying put? We'll keep her safe. I have some ideas on that. Security measures, courtesy of my company. It would keep Franny where she is, but under constant surveillance so nothing happens to her. If Deputy Campbell stays where he's at, he can man the surveillance. Keep an eye out for Franny."

"And find whoever it is threatening her, thus leading you to Albennie," Royal supplied.

Simmons flicked a glance at him. "More or less."

"You're asking Franny to be your bait?" Beckett demanded. "Not gonna happen."

"Maybe that should be up to Ms. Perkins to decide," Simmons replied with a shrug.

Royal hated that he agreed with Simmons, but it wasn't his place to throw his weight behind anybody. He was essentially just the grunt worker in this situation.

"Simmons is right," the sheriff said. "I know you've got a personal connection, Beckett, but this is the best chance to find that missing woman. And we're not putting Ms. Perkins into any more danger than she stumbled into on her own. What do you think, Campbell?"

All eyes turned to him. Royal wasn't quite sure how he'd jumped into the deep end here, being the rookie and all, but he gave his honest opinion anyway. "I agree with Simmons and Sheriff. Her leaving doesn't do anything but move the target, and not necessarily to a safer place. If Ms. Perkins will agree to it, I think her staying put with new security measures in place is the best option for all of us."

Beckett swore. "Well, someone else is telling her cousins."

Chapter Eleven

Franny was sitting with Audra in the detectives' office when Rosalie stormed in. Duncan wasn't far behind her.

"You shouldn't have called her," Franny muttered. She wasn't sure how she felt about any of this, but Audra and Rosalie feeling the need to mother her grated. It was very near infantilizing.

She could handle this. She could handle being the target of a kidnapper and his creepy threats. Hadn't Audra and Rosalie handled their own dangerous escapades over the past year? Neither one of them was too keen on leaning on help. Why should she be?

"She would have found out in the morning and been furious at both of us for waiting," Audra said, giving Franny's hand a squeeze while Rosalie approached.

"All right. Let's go. I'm taking you back to our place. We've got state-of-the-art security and—"

"No extra beds?" Franny supplied. Because Duncan and Rosalie lived in a cute little cabin on the Kirk Ranch, but it wasn't complete with *guest room*.

"We'll buy one. Rush order. Come on, Franny."

But before she could respond to that in any way, Copeland came in. Followed by the sheriff and Royal.

Everyone, even Audra and Rosalie, looked at the sheriff, waiting for him to explain.

"Ms. Perkins, we've got a request for you. And I know you're surrounded by people who care about you and have concern for your safety, but ultimately the decision is up to you."

"Decision?"

"Mr. Simmons has requested you continue to stay in Hope Town until we have a better lead on the case."

Audra whirled on Copeland. "What is this?" she demanded. And the same time Rosalie said, "Have you taken a blow to the head?" to the *sheriff*.

But it was Royal who answered. "We'll be adding a lot of security options to keep her safe, but we think this is our best chance of stopping this."

"By using her as *bait*?" Audra demanded, still glaring at her fiancé.

Before Copeland could say anything, Rosalie interjected, "I'll stay with her. Personal security. Twenty-four-seven. That's the only way she stays put."

"Sweetheart," Duncan said quietly. "We couldn't even make the drive here without having to pull over so you could throw up."

"Oh, no, Rosalie. Are you sick?" Audra's ire turning to concern as she looked over at her sister. "You shouldn't have come."

Rosalie glared at her husband. "No, I'm not sick."

"Then why would you be… Oh. Oh. *Oh my God!*"

"Oh my *God*," Franny echoed as it dawned on her too.

"Oh my God what?" Copeland demanded irritably.

"She's pregnant," Audra said. Then her eyes filled, and she went and hugged her sister. Franny followed, wrapping her arms around the both of them.

"Oh my God, Rosalie. A *baby*." She rocked with her cousins, overjoyed. Teary herself. But that might be the exhaustion. But a *baby*. It was so sweet. So great. So exciting. So *happy* in the face of all this decidedly unhappy.

"And I would have preferred not to announce that in a damn police station in the middle of the night, so thanks, Ace," Rosalie said glaring at Duncan over Audra and Franny's heads.

"Hey, it's a story. You love those."

"Uh-huh." But she pulled away from the hug, her mouth twisting and the color draining out of her face. "Hell, give me a second." She dashed out from their grasp and then out of the room.

Duncan looked after her a little helplessly. He turned back to them, shrugged. "She's going to want to help, but she's not up to it. The doctor wants her on some anti-nausea medication and she's refusing. She's okay, but she needs to take some extra care of herself, and unfortunately involving herself in this isn't the way to do it."

"She doesn't need to. I'll handle it," Audra said. "I can—"

"You have a ranch to run," Franny told Audra firmly, sad that they had to swing from the happy news of a *baby* to…whatever this was. "Copeland's got work to do. You're busy people with real lives, and this isn't… I'm not saying it's not a concern, but if the sheriff's department is looking out for me, how much safer could I be?" She turned her gaze to Royal. He stood stiff and stoic. Even though he wasn't dressed in his uniform, didn't have that gun belt slung on his waist, he looked like he was holding himself as though he was wearing a uniform.

And he was the reason nothing bad had happened tonight, she was almost sure. If he could do that… "Royal was close enough to stop it before a break-in even happened *before* we knew I might be threatened. I'm even safer now that we know I have been, sort of. I can handle this, Audra."

Audra raised an eyebrow. "Royal, is it?"

Franny shook her head at Audra, not going down that line of questioning. Not right now. She turned her attention to the sheriff.

"Sheriff, I'll stay. I want to do whatever I can to help bring Albennie home."

The sheriff nodded. "You follow instructions, Ms. Perkins, we'll keep you safe. Deputy Campbell is in charge of this for the time being. You have any questions, he's your man. Now, if you'll excuse me."

Which left her in a room with her family. And Royal.

"I can give you guys some time to talk this over," Royal said, sounding very formal and professional. "When you're ready, Ms. Perkins, I'll take you back to your apartment. Mr. Simmons is already working on beefing up the security, but I can assure you all, we won't be leaving her on her own until it's all set up."

"Yes. She won't be on her own because she's going to be with us," Audra said firmly.

"Audra. Please." Franny didn't know how to argue with Audra. It went against all her people-pleasing tendencies. But this was…important. The police wanted her to stay, and she wanted to…help. Like she hadn't been able to help when she'd watched Albennie get dragged into that car.

"You cannot just…handle this on your own," Audra said. "It's insane the police are even asking you to. Don't be stubborn for the sake of being stubborn."

"Pot. Kettle."

All eyes turned to Copeland, who'd assuredly taken his

own life into his hands with those words. But he didn't back down.

"It's true. The both of you know it," he said, pointing at Audra then Rosalie as she came back into the room. "You're two of the most hardheaded women I've ever known, and I deal with criminals for a living. At least your cousin has the sense to accept *help* without putting up a fuss. That's more than I can say for the two of you when threats come knocking."

Audra and Rosalie scowled at him, but they didn't mount arguments. Because there was no argument to be mounted.

"And Franny is right. Deputy Campbell is right across the street. With the security precautions Simmons is adding, there's no reason to believe Franny won't be safe. Safer there, with surveillance and a cop always on duty in Hope Town—twenty-four-seven—than at the ranch with just you and me. Or even at the Kirk Ranch. Isolated, far away from town."

The room was silent for a few humming minutes. Audra turned to Franny. "I don't like it."

Franny met her cousin's gaze. "I didn't ask you to."

Audra closed her eyes and shook her head, but that was how Franny knew she'd won.

ROYAL WAS CHOKING down some dregs of coffee that had probably been made twelve hours before and had since kind of burned at the bottom of the pot. But it was the only thing keeping him awake at the moment.

Everything was taken care of on his end—Beckett would handle the evidence. Simmons was off getting the security arrangements ready. He couldn't ask the businesses for their security footage until actual morning.

So he was just standing around waiting for Franny to

be done with her family so he could take her back to her apartment.

He understood her cousins' reservations. He understood their desire to save and protect.

Brooke had tried to protect him like that. He'd never appreciated it. He wondered why he couldn't accept it back then when he'd needed it most. Why now, when he didn't need anyone protecting him, he could look back and understand what she'd been doing and appreciate it.

Life was a hell of a ride.

He looked up from his coffee mug at the sound of footsteps. Franny stepped in, looking back over her shoulder with some concern.

He dumped the terrible coffee, rinsed out the mug. "Ready to go?"

She nodded. "I distracted Audra with baby talk and ran, so we might want to hurry."

He chuckled, led her back outside. There was the hint of a sunrise on the horizon as they got into his car. At first, they drove in silence.

He didn't really know what to say to her. He wanted to offer reassurances, but then wondered if that was too personal. And she wasn't sitting there airing her worries, so maybe she wasn't worried. Maybe she had it all under control.

He flicked a glance at the way her hands were gripped in her lap. Like all her stress was centered there.

Yeah, she didn't have it under control. She probably needed a good night's sleep and a decent meal. Then she'd have the reserves to deal. She *had* agreed to stay, and not everyone would be brave enough to do that.

Should he tell her she was brave? While he was trying to decide, she sighed.

"I love watching the sunrise here," she said as they drove toward the one bleeding out in front of them. "I rarely do it, because I also love morning sleep, but… It's different here, isn't it?"

He looked at the little sliver of sun peeking its way over the horizon, the colors in bright pinks and oranges slashing out across the sky. He glanced at her, because the sunrise looked the same to him no matter where he was. But he didn't want to argue. "Sure."

She *almost* chuckled. "Maybe you're just so used to it you don't know. Did you grow up here?"

Uncomfortable, Royal didn't allow himself to shift. He kept his gaze resolutely on the road. "No."

"Where'd you grow up?"

"Why are you interrogating me all of a sudden?"

"I'm not trying to interrogate you. I'm trying to stay awake." She blew out a breath. "And not think about how on edge I'm going to be in my apartment knowing someone tried to break in."

"So why'd you agree to this?"

She turned that gaze on him, and he *refused* to meet it. Not because he was a coward, but because he was *driving*. Obviously.

But she repeated the question. "Where'd you grow up, Royal?" she demanded this time.

He sighed. He didn't want to talk about *growing up*, but if she was going to be stubborn about it… "South Dakota."

"Ooh, the Mount Rushmore state."

"Never been."

She leaned forward, staring at him. "You grew up in South Dakota and never went to Mount Rushmore?"

You don't tend to go to tourist sights when you spend most of your childhood in a dangerous biker gang. It was on the tip of his tongue to say it. Not just to shock her, but because he was curious how she'd react.

But not *that* curious. "There weren't a lot of family vacations when I was growing up." Unless moving from outskirt nomad campsite to outskirt nomad campsite counted. Unless the one nice foster family he'd been with taking him to their biological kid's baseball game in Brookings counted. Which hadn't been half bad, compared to all the other stuff in his life.

But it wasn't Mount Rushmore.

"Well, next time you go home to visit you'll have to rectify that," Franny said, as if he had a home to go visit. "It's great. We went when I was like…twelve, I think. I loved it. Of course, I was a little history nerd."

"Yeah, well, I've got no plans to return." Maybe his father was in jail, for good this time. Maybe the Sons were dead and buried. But there was nothing for Royal back in South Dakota except bad memories.

He could feel her studying him. He could practically hear gears in her head turning, deciding what question to ask next. If she wasn't such an odd little thing, she'd probably make a good detective.

But he didn't want to be studied, asked or figured out. So he went on the offensive.

"Why'd you agree to this, Franny?"

She looked hard at the road in front of them, or maybe that sunrise she thought was so different in Wyoming. "I watched Albennie get shoved into that car. I watched and I didn't do anything." She didn't say it with a hitch to her voice. She was very firm, very matter-of-fact. "Now it's been days, and nothing I *did* do has helped find her or bring her home. So, if I can do something, even if it's scary or a bit dangerous, I'm going to do it."

He understood, better than most people, what it felt like to witness terrible things, and to have no recourse. He'd spent a lot of time blaming himself pretty hard for that, but Franny shouldn't. She was just…a good person. A *normal* person. Not like him. "What could you have done?" he asked gently, because he wanted her to really think about that.

Sometimes bad things happened, and no matter what you *wanted*, there was no way to fix that.

"I don't know," she said, leaning back in her seat. "Maybe nothing. But now I *can* do something. So I'm going to do it."

Despite her clasped hands, the exhaustion written plain on her face, she said that with conviction.

"And I'm going to keep you safe while you do," he promised.

Because *this* was why he'd let Brooke talk him into the police academy. *Protecting* was why he was here.

He wasn't about to fail at that.

Chapter Twelve

Franny felt like she was in a movie. Mr. Simmons and his partner, a man he'd introduced as Cam Delaney, were doing all sorts of things to her apartment that felt more suited for a spy.

They'd already done most of it by the time Royal walked her up to her apartment, and Mr. Simmons gave her the rundown while Mr. Delaney finished up.

"As you know, there was already a security system in place, but we beefed it up. Now, do you know what the first step to any security system being successful is?" Mr. Simmons asked her.

She blinked at him—not sure if it was ignorance or exhaustion that made her mind completely blank.

"Turning it on," he finished—some censure in his tone, but it wasn't unkind.

"I do! Before I go to bed." When he raised an eyebrow, she wrinkled her nose. "I just hadn't gone to bed yet last night."

"Now you turn it on at all times, even if you're inside and awake. We've made the doorbell camera more sensitive, and we're going to connect it not just to your phone but to Deputy Campbell's as well. On top of that, we've added another camera—this one hidden—that encompasses the entire doorway and stairway. All video will be available to Deputy Campbell and the sheriff—in real time, and as video later on. Should they decide they want to add anyone else who can access that, that'll be up to them, but they'll have to disclose that information to you."

Right. Cameras. Security. All for her safety.

"You've got a camera set up in this living area," Mr. Simmons continued, pointing to a little square on the top of her bookshelf that she barely noticed. "It will pick up sound. Obviously for privacy we've left any equipment out of the bedroom and bathroom, but we've added cameras on the outside of the building at each window point, and more sensitivity to the window alarms. I went ahead and bolted the bathroom window shut, as that seemed the best security option there. All alarms will be connected to the deputy's phone, so that he can respond as needed. Deputy, I'll need your phone to program that real quick."

"Sure," Royal said, fishing the phone out of his pocket and handing it over to Mr. Simmons.

Cameras. In her house. It was for her safety, but the idea of Royal and the sheriff being able to watch her, like, cook *dinner* was not exactly one she relished. Still, she had to admit it would give her a certain level of reassurance no one was trying to get in her door—and if they *were*, someone would stop them before it happened.

"It's a lot, and it's going to feel awkward. I don't think anyone expects this to be easy or feel normal," Mr. Simmons said, frowning at Royal's phone as his fingers moved across the screen.

"If it might help catch whoever has Albennie or took her, then I don't care how it feels," Franny replied, happy she sounded surer of that than she was.

Mr. Simmons smiled warmly as he handed Royal his phone back. "Good. Now there is one more thing. This one is optional. Up to you and Deputy Campbell here." He pulled out two cases. They looked like earbud cases.

"These are a bit like a walkie-talkie, in layman's terms. Let's say Ms. Perkins heads down to the bakery while Deputy Campbell is driving out to the Temperance Ranch for a disturbance call. You both have one of these in your ears, and you can talk to each other—and only each other—without anyone having to know that's what you're doing. They're small. They're wired to only each other. How and when you'd want to use them are up to you, but it'd give you a direct line to each other if you need that."

He handed them out and Royal and Franny had no choice but to each take one.

"I'm going to go do one last sight check on the outside cameras. Call if you need anything, including tech support. Franny? You set that system once Deputy Campbell leaves."

Franny nodded, looking at the little case in her hands. It was like being a spy, except all of her privacy was being invaded. She couldn't—wouldn't—complain about that. She knew what she was doing it for.

She looked over at Royal sheepishly. "I guess we're about to be ear buddies." *Ear buddies. Oh my God, Franny Perkins, what is* wrong *with you?*

Royal smiled—which was really very kind of him considering how ridiculous she sounded. "I'm glad it's an option. I want you wearing them anytime you leave the apartment. Just text me your schedule."

Franny nodded. "Right. Sure." Maybe she'd just never leave the apartment again.

"I've got to get going. I'm going to be late for my shift."

She trailed after him to the door. "But you didn't sleep."

"I got a few hours before you called me. It's okay. Part of the job."

"Royal…" She didn't know what to say. *Thank you* seemed so lame. *I'm terrified* was definitely not his problem.

Royal gestured down to where Mr. Simmons stood with Mr. Delaney, discussing something underneath her back window. "Did you know he's married to Daisy Delaney?" Royal asked.

Franny blinked at the odd segue, but then she nodded. "My friend Vi? Her husband is friends with Mr. Simmons, so she *met* her."

"So did I. She was in my apartment. Foisted a baby off on Simmons while he was getting me set up." Royal shook his head. "Hell of a thing."

"I desperately want to ask her a million questions for a million book ideas, but that feels pretty… I don't know. Crass." And it was nice, to end this strange interlude on something that wasn't threats and fear.

She supposed that's why he'd brought it up.

"Crass," he repeated. Then shook his head. "I've got to go. You should get some sleep. I'll come back tonight after my shift, and we'll talk about how…all this works."

She nodded. "Yeah. That sounds good."

"You're worried about something, you call me. You need to leave after you've gotten some rest, text me. We'll try these out." He held up the earbud case.

"Got it."

"And remember to—"

"Set the security. I know, I know." She tried to smile at him. "I appreciate…all of this."

"You appreciate having your life upended by witnessing a crime?"

She laughed in spite of herself. "No. Not even a little. But I do appreciate what everyone is trying to do to bring Albennie home and keep me safe in the midst of it."

Royal jogged down the stairs, hoping he'd be able to catch Simmons before he left. There were things he wanted to discuss without Franny hearing.

Not that she didn't deserve to know everything, but he needed to make sure his suspicions were on the right track, and he wanted to get a better sense of Zach Simmons.

That story back in the sheriff's office, about women who came here to hide from pasts, it made sense. Hell, he knew firsthand just how complicated pasts could be. Simmons's information explained the predominance of women, the businesses leased to *only* women. It explained a lot.

And if it was true, Royal couldn't help but respect it. It was a hell of an idea. He could have used it for a few of the girls stuck in the Sons' life.

But it also led them to where they were now, which was putting Franny in danger all because she'd *seen* something. Because he'd leased her an apartment to add "normal" people to the town.

It wasn't right.

Simmons was at the back of the building now. His partner was nowhere to be seen. Which was good. Royal wanted to keep as many things on the down-low as possible.

"Simmons, I need to talk to you."

"Sure. Have at."

"This break-in, this threat. Is it my imagination, or is the timing suspicious?"

"Suspicious how?" Simmons asked, poking at something on his phone then looking up at the roof of the building. Presumably checking different security checkpoints.

"Somebody shows up at Franny's door *after* the car she IDed is found in Idaho. The Feds, allegedly, pull out of Wyoming to focus on Idaho."

"Likely the kidnapper ditched the car in Idaho, then doubled back here to make his threat."

"Likely, yeah. But only if that meant they'd dropped Albennie Ward off with someone." He didn't come out and say *if she was still alive*. Royal figured her being dead was just as possible, but he also knew that sometimes kidnapping people for information or ransom was a more complicated endeavor.

He assumed whatever past Albennie Ward had leaned more to that than quick, easy murder. Otherwise someone would have taken her out here.

"What's your point, Deputy?"

"My point is, this only makes sense if the guy who kidnapped Albennie was for hire. He drops off the kidnapping victim, ditches the car, but he knows he's got a loose end. The woman who saw him. I'm worried even when we get him, he'll have no connection to the real brain behind this, and we'll be exactly where we are right now, except Franny will be safer."

Simmons was quiet for a long humming moment. "I don't love that theory, deputy, I've got to say."

"Then what's yours?"

"Runs similar to yours at first. Yeah, I'd wager a bet he's a kidnapper for hire. He drops Albennie off with whoever actually wanted her. There's no on-paper connection." Simmons shrugged like that was obvious. "But when we catch him? There's no honor amongst thieves, Campbell. None that I've seen. He'll talk, and it'll lead us to whoever really has Albennie."

"If you have the right kind of ringleader, loyalty is a hell of a drug. It's not honor amongst thieves, it's…belief." He thought of the way his father had worshipped Ace Wyatt, leader of the Sons. Like the man was God himself. His dad would have done *anything* for Ace. Kept any secret, weathered any punishment, because he'd believed that someday, somewhere, there'd be something in it for him.

"You know what else is a hell of a drug?" Simmons asked. "Threat of the death penalty."

"For kidnapping?"

Simmons sighed, shoving his phone into his pocket. "That's where things are…tricky." He started walking to his car, so Royal fell into step next to him.

"The Feds know who did this, don't they?"

"Know? No. Have some ideas? Yeah, that's my take, but as many friends as I have, as many strings as I can pull, I'm not FBI any longer. I don't have access to everything they know. I can only wager some guesses based on how things have gone, based on what little information I was given when Albennie came here."

"So, when are they going to come back?"

"They're not."

"What?"

"They don't know about the break-in. If I can help it, they won't."

"Why the hell not?" Royal demanded. He wasn't too thrilled with the Feds keeping things from local police, but he happened to feel like right now the more law enforcement agencies were working on this, the better.

"Because I'm starting to worry that Albennie's location was leaked somewhere on their side of things. It shouldn't have been possible for anyone from her past to find her. So unless she gave herself away, which I just can't fathom, it's there. Somewhere in there."

"Then why'd you involve them in the first place?"

Simmons just spared him a look.

"It's complicated. Right," Royal muttered. But it made him remember the strange woman he'd assumed was a

Fed. "Did you know all the agents who were here after the kidnapping?"

"Not all of them personally."

"But you know. Who should be here. Who shouldn't."

Simmons narrowed his eyes. "Sure. Or I could find out. Why?"

"What about a brunette, brown eyes, mid-thirties. Five-six, a buck twenty, maybe more. She had some muscle on her. A tiny trio of moles on her chin, and I *think* a birthmark, faint, on the back of her neck."

"That doesn't describe anyone I can think of off the top of my head, but I can poke into it deeper."

"I've got footage of her on my body cam."

"If you send me that or a still of the woman, I'll look into it. But you'd have to trust me to do that."

Royal wondered why he did. What had changed. He supposed everything this man had said in the sheriff's office this morning. And how he'd handled Franny's security now. "All that stuff up there, you claim only the sheriff and I have access to it."

"I don't just claim. It's true. Professional guarantee. Not saying I don't have the skills to hack into anything if I had a mind to, but CD Corp is on the up and up. You could hire an unbiased third party to make sure of it, but it'd take time and I sure as hell hope this is done soon."

"Yeah, me too."

"Look, Deputy, I get the suspicion. Respect it even. Law enforcement requires a certain level of it. I know that from experience. But my entire goal is to bring Albennie Ward back home without anyone getting hurt."

Royal's gaze tracked up to Franny's apartment. "Yeah, mine too. I'll send you that picture."

Chapter Thirteen

Franny did sleep. It wasn't a great, restful sleep but it was sleep nonetheless. She couldn't seem to drag herself out of bed until late afternoon—half dozing and half worrying the day away. Then she tried to read, to write, to watch a movie on her computer, but her mind kept wandering to the cameras surveilling her apartment.

Eventually, her stomach demanded sustenance, cameras be damned. It was nearly seven by the time she felt presentable enough to be *constantly video monitored* and shuffled out into the living area.

She needed to make herself a decent dinner, not just do what she wanted to do and eat chips and maybe a block of cheese. She opened her pantry and then refrigerator, surveying the contents.

"Spaghetti it is," she said out loud, then nearly groaned remembering she was on *surveillance* and anyone who watched or listened would in fact *observe* her talking to herself. *Fantastic.*

Irritated and jumpy, she set about making dinner. She wanted to turn some music on, or the TV, anything to drown out the sound of her own thoughts screaming: *you are being recorded*, but what if someone came up the stairs? What if another threat came?

What if, God forbid, she started *dancing and singing along* to something?

And even if she didn't need to be listening for a threat or constantly monitoring her own behavior, Royal would be coming whenever his shift was done. Which should be soon, shouldn't it? Maybe she should make enough spaghetti for him.

She stared at the boiling water, debating her choices. She stopped herself from saying *to hell with it* out loud and dumped the entire contents of the box in the water. If she had enough leftover spaghetti for a week, so be it.

The *least* she could do was offer him some food when he came by. So she focused on putting together a decent dinner. Made some garlic toast with what pieces of bread she had left. Her only vegetable option was a can of green beans that didn't exactly go with the rest, but hey, it was green.

She was just straining the pasta when her text notification went off. She glanced at the screen. From Royal.

On my way up.

She looked at the text, then at the door. There was no reason to be nervous. Or feel weird. She was going to eat dinner. He could join if he wanted while they discussed strategy, or he could watch her eat while they did.

Either way, this was her life now. She crossed to the door, disengaged the alarm, then opened it.

He'd changed into a T-shirt and shorts. His hair was damp like he'd run through the shower before he'd come over. He stepped inside and closed the door behind him, then he gestured toward the door, a nonverbal *set the alarm again*.

She did, even though it felt a bit like being in *jail*, but that was the price to pay for safety and she was determined to be reasonable about that.

"I was just finishing up making dinner. Spaghetti. If you're hungry, you can…have some. There's plenty."

"Oh—" He glanced at the kitchen, and she couldn't quite read the expression on his face, but she was worried it was discomfort. Like he felt *bad* for her and would *pity* accept.

"But you don't have to. Just extra, if you want. If you're hungry. I'm going to eat, because I'm hungry." Jeez, she was a mess.

"Well, sure. I…haven't eaten yet."

"Great," she replied, no doubt sounding *far* too cheerful. She walked back to the kitchen, finished up preparations then handed him a plate. "Help yourself. What would you like to drink? I've got water. A variety of zero-calorie pops. And milk that expired three days ago."

He chuckled a little at that. "Water's fine."

It was very awkward to share the tiny kitchen space with someone so…big. He smelled like soap and she was having a hard time not cataloguing all the tattoos on his arm when what she needed to do was get him a glass of water and get her own dinner sorted.

Once that was finally done, they took a seat at the little dining table that had come with the apartment or she wouldn't have bothered with. She preferred to eat on the couch. Or in bed.

Now she sat across from Royal eating very basic spaghetti and canned green beans at her kitchen table.

"So, I'm on duty seven to seven here in Hope Town. Deputy Mayfield handles the night shift." He covered his spaghetti in an alarming amount of the parmesan she'd put on the table. "Simmons has all the alarms connected into my phone, so anything that happens should wake me up even overnight. Plus, I've got my phone set so a call or text from you goes through no matter what."

"What about days off?"

"Usually it'd be weekends, but Sheriff and I thought it'd be best to just work through this. Ideally, we get to the bottom of things before I work too many days in a row. What about your schedule?"

She was stuck for a moment, not sure if she was supposed to insist he take days off or if she should just accept that he and the sheriff were doing the right thing. It's not like this was *for* her exactly. It was to find Albennie.

"Well, I usually like to go down to the bakery for my afternoon coffee and baked good, but I certainly don't have to anymore. At some point this week I probably need to go to the grocery store. But I can really just...hermit down with the best of them."

His mouth curved into an almost...half smile. It was kind but not patronizing. Kind of like she *amused* him, in a good way.

She didn't know what the hell to do with that. So she ate her dinner and they worked out how they'd handle surveillance monitoring. When he'd be watching, when they should wear the earbuds.

It wasn't that complicated, all in all. *Weird?* Yes. Complicated? No. But they were both still eating once they'd determined the logistics and an uncomfortable kind of lull fell over the table.

Franny didn't know why it was uncomfortable, or why she couldn't seem to think of anything to say except to interrogate him about his life because she was desperately curious.

Was he curious at all about her? *No, because you are not that interesting*. But she had invited him to dinner, and he was *protecting her*, so it was probably her job to keep conversation going.

Or you just want to know about him. "So you grew up in South Dakota. Your sister is a forensic anthropologist and you're a cop. Law enforcement run in the family?"

He laughed, not an amused laugh but a full-on maybe even a little caustic laugh. "No. Not at all."

She knew a red light when she saw one. Curiosity was a hard thing for her to tamp down, but she did when she knew the questions weren't wanted, wouldn't be welcomed. She was uncomfortable enough in her own skin half the time, she hated to make anyone else feel uncomfortable.

But just because she knew she couldn't ask all the questions she wanted to didn't mean she knew what to say. So another awkward silence descended.

"Why do you have so many questions about me, Franny?" Royal asked her.

For a moment she just met his gaze, her heart fluttering around in her chest. The truth was, she always had questions about people, but she didn't always *voice* those questions. Not everyone interested her.

He did. For a lot of reasons. But she wasn't going to tell him *that*.

"People are interesting," she said, trying to sound casual. "People are kind of my job. Writing stories is just…discovering how people tick. I guess sometimes that just slips out into trying to be a normal human being making conversation. And if you haven't gathered, normal isn't one of my top qualities."

His mouth curved, ever so slightly. But his blue eyes were very serious. "So, if Brooke and I were characters in your book, what would make us tick?"

She could play this a couple different ways. It was a challenge of sorts, she could recognize that, though she didn't know what he was hoping to gain from the challenge. So she just told him the truth.

"Well, based on the way you laughed at me asking if your family was in law enforcement, and the fact that you were quite adamant you'd never want to go back to South Dakota, my fictionalized version of that childhood—which is usually what makes people tick—would be…raised by criminals, saw awful things, so grew up wanting to protect people. Because you weren't protected when you were vulnerable."

He studied her for a long time. Long enough she had to look away or she'd start blushing. Or start staring *very* hard at the tattoo on his right bicep that peeked out under his T-shirt sleeve.

It looked like the bottom half of a heart, and she desperately wanted to know if it had something inside like: *Mom* or a woman's name.

What kind of woman would prompt Royal to get her name tattooed on his arm?

When he finally spoke, it was with a kind of gravity that had her looking back up.

"Maybe your fictions aren't far off." He downed a gulp of water like it was hard liquor that might take the sting away. He set the glass down, fixed her with that intense stare of his. "You ever heard of the Sons of the Badlands?"

She blinked once, swallowed, feeling unaccountably nervous and not really sure why. Except, she supposed, nothing about the Sons of the Badlands was *good* conversation. "The biker gang cult group?"

"Yeah. What do you know about them?"

"Well, uh, my second book, the reason I first came to live with Audra and Rosalie in fact, was because I was researching cults to base my fictional one on. I mainly focused on the Order of Truth. That old cult from the seventies that lived out near Sunrise? I was interested in the religious fanaticism and the isolated location, but I wanted something more criminal, so I fell down a little Sons of the Badlands research rabbit hole. For the story, I liked their whole nomad thing, and their broader scope. Much more menacing. Combining the two created a nice fictional hybrid that suited my purposes."

She wasn't surprised he was staring at her a bit like she'd grown a second head. Because she was yammering on about what she liked about *cults* for God's sake. "Fictional purposes, obviously," she tacked on lamely. "That stuff is all interesting to me for my...fictional world." She shut her mouth, because how bizarre must that sound to someone who didn't write?

But Royal didn't look confused or horrified. He still looked very, very serious. "Brooke and I were born into the Sons."

He just...said that. Like it was a normal thing to tell someone. *I was born into a notorious, murderous biker gang.*

"Oh," was all she could think of to say.

"Brooke managed to get us out when I was pretty young, but we got separated and the foster families I was tossed around to weren't much better. So I went back."

Franny nodded along like this was a normal conversation she knew how to deal with. Her with her privileged upper class, only child upbringing.

He studied her, like he was keeping track of every last reaction she had to this information.

"You've got eight million questions, but you won't ask them," he said. "Why? Because it's *crass*?"

She shifted in her chair. That was the word she'd used when they'd discussed Daisy Delaney. It wasn't the only word that applied here, and she wasn't sure what he wanted from her. She wasn't sure what was the right way to deal with this. Maybe just…try to keep it simple.

"Yeah, it is. I like to research. I use a lot of real-life stuff in my books. I follow a lot of…stories and things that interest me because people interest me. But I'm not going to make you uncomfortable to get some questions answered for a book I might write someday. That's not nice or right, and I like to be both. If I can."

She didn't have to tell him she was already thinking about how she could fit it into her current book. Giving her federal agent hero *or* her cop heroine a background of having actually grown up in a cult, or at least something dangerous, had about a million new ideas springing to life.

Maybe that sowed a lot of distrust when they had to work together—the fed didn't trust a cop from such a background? Maybe they both came from horrible backgrounds and bonded over it?

But she wasn't going to let her mind go down that road right now.

He shook his head. "You're just about the strangest woman I ever met."

She felt a little stung and knew that was stupid. But it didn't stop the words from falling out of her mouth. "You are not the first person to say that to me, but I'm not going to lie it's far more insulting coming from a cop that grew up in a biker gang."

Then he laughed. Really laughed. Not caustic or bitter or anything. "Hell, Franny." He shook his head. "I'm not trying to insult you. You're interesting. *I* don't find people very interesting as a whole. I tend to want to know as little about everyone as possible, because more often than not, people suck."

She thought about that. He hadn't really asked any questions about her. Maybe he was right and he didn't have any—considering she had approximately eight million for him.

But…not being interested in people, believing they all sucked, didn't add up. "You wouldn't have gone into helping people if that were totally true."

He looked down at his plate, a puzzled kind of expression on his face. Then he got to his feet. "I should get going. Thanks for dinner. Can I help you clean up?"

Franny shook her head. "No, don't worry about it."

Still he collected his dishes and took them to the sink. For a moment, she just sat there, then she finally pushed herself into a standing position.

Obviously, he'd done what he'd come for. He wasn't just going to hang around all night. He had his own place, and he was probably exhausted since he'd had to work twelve hours today. Not just lie in bed all day like she had.

"I really appreciate not having to make myself a meal for once," he said as he moved for the door.

Right. He really was kind, but it was clear he wanted to head for the hills, and who could blame him?

But he didn't stride right out. He turned and gave her a kind smile. "And the company's not bad."

"Except for the poking into your tragic past, I would assume."

"Pretty sure I gave that up of my own free will. It's not something I just go around telling everyone." He studied her in that intense way of his. She wondered if he did that to criminals or if she was special.

You are not special in this scenario, Franny. A step above criminal maybe, but not special.

"So what's your childhood story? You didn't grow up here."

"No. Washington state. My dad is an engineer. My mother is a math teacher. Aside from being a dreamy, head-in-the-clouds artistic type, which made and makes no sense to my parents at all, I had a very easy, lovely upbringing. Probably even spoiled thanks to my health issues."

He frowned. "Health issues?"

She waved it away. "Oh, it's all sorted now. Just some allergies and asthma. It just took a while to figure out, so I had a few hospital stays when I was very little to freak my parents out. Kinda stuck with all of us. Trauma for them, trauma-lite for me."

"Trauma-lite," he echoed.

"Should we call yours extra-mega trauma?"

He laughed again, the nice one not the harsh one. "Yeah. At the very least. But I guess it makes sense then. I'd rather be a sick head-in-the-clouds dreamer than a sick realist."

It was…shockingly astute. She had used books and fiction and her own little stories to take her mind off her allergy issues growing up.

"And I'd rather be just about anything other than a math teacher," he added.

It made her laugh, because *same*, but then he moved for the door again. He was leaving, and of course he *should*. He needed to. But…

The thought of being there alone with her thoughts and security camera and…everything, it caused a little spiral of panic to move through her.

He reached for the door, and she just couldn't bear the thought.

"What about dessert?" she asked, desperately she could admit. To herself anyway.

But Royal studied her like he fully understood. "You

know, if you're afraid to be alone, you can tell me that. You've every right to be afraid."

"Says the guy who escaped from a biker gang and became a cop."

"Am I going to regret telling you that?"

"Probably." What was the point in pretending? "Why did you?"

"I don't know. I don't know why I do a lot of things when it comes to you." He said it with a smile, but his eyes were serious. They were always serious. And he did tend to look at her…

She didn't have words for it, and she had words for everything. There was just this…weight to it. Like he looked at her and *saw* her.

Surely she…was just imagining things.

"Night, Franny."

She should say good night. He wanted to leave, needed to leave, and she had no right to keep him there.

But…

"Okay, I admit it. I'm afraid. I don't want to be alone in here. It freaks me out. Not just some guy out there wanting to threaten me or worse, but being in here with cameras so you can hear my every talking-to-myself moment if you want to."

"You talk to yourself?"

"I could make cookies," she said, totally desperate now. "And you could just stay a little longer. Just… Please, I know it's silly and intrusive and a million other things you didn't sign up for, but…"

"Sure." He took his hand off the knob. "I like cookies."

Relief swelled through her like a tide, and since she desperately wanted this to be okay, to not be ruining his life, she walked over to the couch, grabbed the remote and handed it to him. "You can watch TV if you want. I've got the streaming services in the first row, and then if you scroll a little bit, I've got a baseball subscription. There should be a few games on tonight."

He took the remote but looked at her dubiously. "*You* like baseball?"

"Why do you say it like that?"

"Because you just don't seem like the type. You told me yourself you're head-in-the-clouds artistic."

"Sure, but sports are stories, Royal. And baseball is stories *and* history. Baseball has marked the *time*."

"Did you just quote *Field of Dreams*?"

"Obviously. Besides, I don't know if you noticed, my cousin-in-law is Duncan Kirk."

"I noticed."

She grinned. "I've got his rookie card. Signed now—though I didn't ask until the wedding was over so as not to be *crass*."

"Well, as long as you weren't that." He narrowed his eyes. "You've got a baseball card collection?"

"Yes. At the ranch. I didn't have room to store it here." Which kept her from talking about all the other collections she had: unicorn figurines, antique toasters, her late grandmother's gigantic salt and pepper shaker collection.

"Well, you're going to have to show it off sometime."

She really wished her heart would stop doing this *fluttering* thing. "Sure. Yeah. I… I better get started on those cookies. It shouldn't take more than fifteen," she said, turning back to the kitchen, hoping she had all the ingredients necessary. She *knew* she had chocolate chips and butter—she always had chocolate chips and butter.

She scrounged enough of everything together to create

a kind of half batch. It was funny how much more relaxed she was with him there.

They were still being filmed. It didn't change anything whether he was here or across the street watching, but it *felt* different. It felt safe. But once he ate some cookies she was going to have to let him go and that filled her with such dread.

Be a grown-up, Franny, she scolded herself as she pulled the cookies out of the oven. She piled them up on a plate.

"Here we..." She trailed off. He sat on her couch, head slightly bowed, though his arms were crossed over his chest. His breathing was steady and even and his eyes were closed.

She stared at him there, sleeping soundly in an upright position on her couch. Poor guy was working overtime just to keep her safe. She knew it was his *job*, but it still felt like he was going a little above and beyond.

She knew that wasn't about *her* personally, but that didn't mean she couldn't have gratitude. Surely not every police officer who would have been assigned to this job would be quite so...kind about it.

She should probably wake him up, but she couldn't bring herself to do it when he seemed so deep in it. She'd just... let him sleep.

Selfish, Franny.

Maybe, but it made her feel better knowing he was there.

So she got some blankets, a pillow, and wrote a little note. Then she turned off the TV and left him there sleeping and went to bed herself.

With the cookies, of course.

ROYAL WOKE IN the dark, a sharp pain his neck, and a bunch of old, ugly memories prickling at the edges of his brain.

Had he really told Franny all that about himself? What the hell had possessed him?

Well, that was easy if uncomfortable. Sympathetic green eyes and that careful way she held herself. It reminded him of someone who'd been beaten—always waiting for the next blow. He didn't think that was her issue. She probably would have mentioned it and not called her "health issues" trauma-lite. But there was something there. A vulnerability she wasn't any good at shoring up.

He should not like her for that alone. You had to be tough to get through life, and she was just…soft.

And sweet.

He blew out a breath, stretching his neck to one side and then the other, before doing a full neck roll.

He didn't have a clue how his life had twisted and turned to wind up here. It felt even more unimaginable when he said things like *born into the Sons* and she said things like *engineer dad and math teacher mom.*

Upper middle class for God's sake.

They didn't have a thing in common, and yet he found her endlessly fascinating. She was just…unique, and there was something about her curiosity, her bravery in the face of all this that life had in no way prepared her for, and the open vulnerability that drew those protective instincts he'd honed somewhere along the way.

You either wanted to protect or you wanted to be the monster. Those were the only two options in the life he'd been born into. He didn't consider himself that great of a guy, but he'd never had any interest in being the monster. He supposed that was the only thing that had led him *here.*

That and Brooke. He'd learned to forgive his sister—and it wasn't as though she'd done anything to him that she needed his forgiveness for. It was just he'd gotten through his adolescence and some of his young adulthood by blaming her, by thinking she'd had it better somehow. The grudge had been a crutch.

And it had taken some work to get over it, just like it had taken some work to accept all the people ready and willing to help him build a real life outside of everything that had happened to him and everything he'd done.

He knew those people were *willing* because of Brooke, but getting to know his sister as an adult these past two years had made him fully understand why anyone and everyone rallied around Brooke.

She was a good, kind person. It was at the very core of who she was. No time in the Sons or in a crappy foster home had dulled that.

He wasn't sure he'd ever had it to be dulled.

Franny had it. It was the only explanation for him telling her about the Sons.

He'd *seen* the questions building up inside her, but she hadn't voiced a one. She would, he thought. In the next few days, she wouldn't be able to resist. He could have offered more, explained it deeper.

He'd wanted her to see only the surface of it. A stop sign.

Because it felt a bit like they were on a strange precipice. Neither quite sure what to do with each other. Both a little too...attracted.

Polar opposites. Maybe it made sense. Not that he should *let* it make sense. He should be erecting very clear boundaries to a very complicated and odd situation.

Instead, he had...fallen asleep on her couch. The lights were out but the glow from the microwave clock allowed him to make out the shadows of furniture. He could smell cookies, but the scent was faint.

Hell, how long had he been out? He pulled his phone out

of his pocket. Four. He'd slept for like…at least six hours. He shook his head and clicked on the phone flashlight. On the coffee table in front of him were a stack of blankets and a pillow with a little piece of paper on top.

He picked up the note, read it in the light of his phone.

Royal,
I thought it best to let you sleep. Text me when you need to leave, and I'll get up to set the security system. Otherwise, I set my alarm for six and I'll wake you up so you can get to your shift. Feel free to use whatever you need. Bathroom is in the hall.
—Franny

Like he wouldn't have known who'd written the note. Which made him smile, but not as much as the little PS at the end.

I'm sorry, but I ate all the cookies.

It was four in the morning. It'd be silly to wake her up now to set her security system. He might as well just try to get another hour or two of sleep on the couch.

He grabbed the pillow and tossed it behind him. He didn't bother with the blanket. Even though he could hear the air-conditioning working, it was hot up here.

He lay back and stretched out. He was usually a little too big for a couch, but this was a good size. Cushy. They pillow smelled fresh and clean, kind of like her. He looked up at the dark ceiling.

What the hell was he doing? Getting in way too deep, that was for sure.

Which was just impetus to see this through. Get it done.

Once Albennie Ward was found and it was certain Franny was out of danger, they'd go back to passing each other on the street or bumping into each other at the bakery every *once* in a while.

Things wouldn't feel quite so…tenuous then. He was sure of it.

Almost.

Chapter Fourteen

Franny woke up to her alarm and groaned. She turned it off immediately wondering whose bright idea it was to set it for six in the damn—

She sat bolt right up in bed. If her alarm was going off, Royal had…slept on her couch. Had he woken up at some point and decided to stay? Or had he slept in that horrible upright position?

Was she going to have to wake him up? She couldn't let him be late for work. Not after he'd been so kind as to *stay*.

God, she'd slept so much better knowing he was there. Did that make her pathetic? Well, she was alive and not kidnapped so maybe she didn't care if she was a little pathetic.

What she did care about was having to go out there and wake him up. That was just…awkward.

But she could hardly let him be late for work. She threw the covers off her. She ran her hands through her hair, trying to tame it as she moved around trying to find some clothes. She didn't have a mirror in here. Why didn't she have a mirror in here?

Six in the morning was never her friend, so running around grabbing random items of clothes and then rejecting them wasn't what she *wanted* to be doing, but usually she didn't have to actually *think* before a cup of coffee.

She finally pulled on a pair of yoga pants and an oversized T-shirt. She was about to open her door when she stopped herself.

"Bra. My God, Franny, put on a bra." Thank God there were no cameras in here. She backtracked, put on a bra, and then took a deep breath, let it out.

This was not the panic-inducing moment she was making it out to be.

Rolling her eyes at herself, she opened her bedroom door and stepped out into the hallway. She heard the faint sound of movement and edged into the main area.

Royal was standing, looking at something on his phone—the light from it and the hint of early sunlight from around the blinds were the only things illuminating the room.

Unerringly he looked up at her when she took one more step.

She held her hand up in the most awkward wave of all time then turned the main overhead light on. She managed a smile, hoped it didn't read as awkward as it felt. "Morning."

"Morning," he said, his voice gruff. Which was hot. Because he was hot. And she could not be thinking about *that* right now.

"I know it's silly, but I slept *way* better knowing you were here, so I really appreciate your willingness to humor me."

He shoved his phone in his pocket and put the pillow on the stack of blankets he hadn't used. "I appreciate you not waking me up. Probably got a solid eight in. Your couch isn't half bad."

"Good."

He made a gesture for the door. "I better get back to my place so I can be ready for my shift on time. Just text me if you plan on going somewhere. Sound good?"

She nodded.

Before he could move, or she could offer coffee or breakfast or something, a knock sounded at the door. They both looked at it, then froze. Neither making a move one way or another.

Maybe he was as little of a morning person as she was, because he didn't immediately tell her what to do or do anything himself.

"Well, kidnappers don't really knock, right?" She managed a shaky kind of laugh and moved for the door. "I'll look out and see who it is." She moved to her toes, looked out the peephole.

It was… Copeland. She fell to her heels. She didn't dare look back at Royal. This looked… Well, surely Copeland wouldn't jump to weird conclusions. He'd understand.

But she was *nervous* now. "Uh, it's Copeland," she offered. Then disengaged the alarm and unlocked the door.

"Franny, sorry for the…" His gaze tracked beyond her to Royal, his expression immediately hardening. "What the hell are you doing here at six thirty in the morning?"

"Protecting me," Franny said firmly. She stepped between Copeland's angry gaze and Royal. "Remember?"

"Yeah, how far is that going?" Copeland demanded of Royal.

"It's not…going." Franny couldn't look at Royal or she'd turn beet red. "And even if it was, absolutely none of your business, Copeland."

"Look—"

"I know you and Audra have a very sweet meet cute from protecting her, but this isn't…that. So stop making things *weird* and explain to me why *you* are here at six thirty in the morning."

He was still glaring at Royal, kind of like the older

brother she never had, which was almost sweet. If she didn't feel so damn embarrassed. He stepped inside and she closed the door behind him.

Then his gaze moved to her, and there was an alarming kind of…regret there. "I just got some…disturbing news. I wanted to tell you in person. Both of you. Didn't imagine you'd both be together, but—" He sighed. "There was a fire this morning at the library in Sunrise. The fire department called me once they saw what was being burned."

"Which was?" Royal demanded, speaking for the first time since Copeland stepped in the door.

"A stack of your books, Franny."

She leaned against the door, slowly let out her exhale as if she could control her breath she could control the jump of fear in her chest. "Well, that's not good."

"If it was burned, how do they know they were Franny's?" Royal asked.

"It's possible they weren't *all* Franny's titles," Copeland said. "But…there was enough left of some of the covers it feels…likely they all were. I talked to the librarian. You know Dahlia, right?" he asked Franny.

She nodded. She liked the librarian out in Sunrise. The library was tiny, but they had a lot of information on the Order of Truth, so she had spent some time there researching that book.

"She said all your books that the library carries were checked out the day before by someone who claimed they were new to Sunrise and got a library card. So, we've got something to go off of. But it is another threat, and I want you both aware of it."

"Why the Sunrise library?" Royal asked. "The Bent County library in Fairmont would have more of her books, wouldn't they?"

"Yes, but if I had to guess, the size of the library worked in the suspect's favor. No surveillance, minimal security. Dahlia can describe the person who got the library card to us, and she will, but…"

"It'll be like me describing the kidnapper. It'll do a fat lot of nothing," Franny said with some level of disgust.

"Or it doesn't. We just don't know." Copeland glanced at her. "I want you to be aware so you're always making an informed decision. If you want to come to the ranch, or have Audra—"

"I think we all know and agree that the safest place for me is here with all this security," Franny managed. "Audra has enough on her plate even with your help, as do all of you. I'm staying put."

Copeland eyed Royal. "Well, if anything changes, you let me know."

"Was it a man or woman?" Royal asked, seemingly out of the blue. "The person who got the library card."

Copeland looked at Royal. There was distrust in his eyes, but eventually he answered. "Dahlia said it was a woman. I'm going to run the information she gave, but I don't have much hope there. Why?"

"Just need to know who to look out for. Is there going to be a sketch?"

Copeland nodded. "She's going to come by the police station this morning. I'll make sure you and Mayfield get a copy of it, and whatever we work up on the ID, even if it's fake."

"As soon as you can," Royal said. "And any other information you get."

"I will. I need to get into the station. Walk me out, Deputy."

Since Copeland didn't say it as a request, Franny felt like

she had to step in. Even if she felt a little out-of-body trying to wrap her mind around someone burning her *books*, she had to protect Royal from…whatever Copeland thought he was doing. "He's not going to walk you out because you're going to do some ridiculous male law enforcement posturing, and I don't want any part of it."

"That's why we're going to do it outside."

"No, you're not." She put her hands on Copeland's chest and gave him a shove. "Bye."

He scowled down at her, but she watched him relent. "I'll have those sketches to you as soon as I've got them, Campbell. Franny, if anything changes—"

"*Bye*, Copeland."

"Bye," he muttered, and turned on his heel and stalked out the door.

Franny locked the door behind him, then stayed staring at the door trying to breathe through the tears that threatened. She wasn't going to cry in front of Royal. She wasn't going to feel *helpless* when she had all these people looking out for her.

"Well, that's…not great." She turned and tried to smile at Royal. "But I guess it doesn't change much for me. Does it?"

"It's a step. Every time they do something, there's a chance they leave clues behind. So, it's actually good."

"Good?" She wanted to believe that, but she knew he was mostly just saying it to set her mind at ease.

"Look, Franny, I have a theory. I'm going to work on getting to the bottom of it."

"Why didn't you tell Copeland this theory?"

Royal studied the door, then moved his gaze back to her. "I want to talk to Simmons first. It's not that I don't trust… your friend there. I just think we have to be more careful.

Sometimes when a lot of people know something, even a lot of well-meaning cops, everything gets too complicated."

"You trust Mr. Simmons?"

"I don't know. I guess I'm starting to."

Franny chewed on her bottom lip, trying to work through *any* of this, but… He had to get to work. And she should probably try to get some work done too. She unlocked the door, opened it for him, and tried to force her mouth to curve upward. "Thanks again for last night."

He nodded, moving for the door. But he stopped, reached out, but his big hand on her shoulder and squeezed. "It's going to be okay, Franny."

"Of course," she said brightly.

But she figured they were both lying.

ROYAL GOT READY in a rush. He tried not to think about how…down Franny had looked when he'd left. She had every right to be worried *and* down, and it wasn't his job to cheer her up.

The fact he wanted to make it all right for her was completely and utterly foreign. He'd just never before believed he could make something awful *right*. Better maybe. Put a stop to something terrible. But not actually make it right.

There had been too much awful all around him to ever make right.

But Franny hadn't grown up like that, and he found himself…needing to fix this so she didn't have to live with any *bad* hanging on her shoulders.

He shook his head as he let himself into his temporary apartment. That was a little ridiculous. He needed to… screw his head on straight today. Focus on the case. He couldn't decide if this was an escalation of threat—sure, fire was worse than a piece of paper, but the piece of paper had been on her doorstep. The fire had been miles away.

Though it didn't really matter what *he* thought, did it? It mattered what the person doing the threats thought. And he had the background to know that even if you *thought* you understood a bad person, that understanding could change on a dime.

The fact it was a woman bothered him. And that so easily could be a coincidence, but… It just didn't feel like one. He should call the sheriff. Hell, call Beckett. But Simmons worrying about leaks left Royal needing to be cautious.

He was probably being overly paranoid. But if there was anything his childhood had taught him it was to listen to all those looming *bad* gut feelings. It usually meant something was wrong.

Simmons had said he'd get in touch once he had information on the picture of the woman. And if she *was* a Fed, it'd be something for Simmons to look into, not him. But what if she wasn't? What was next?

Royal worked through that question as he did his Hope Town patrol duties.

It was nearing lunchtime when he saw Simmons was pushing a giant stroller down the sidewalk toward the bakery Royal had considered hitting up.

Maybe as an excuse to text Franny and ask her if she wanted anything.

So he was pretty glad for the distraction, because that would have been foolish and unnecessary. He'd spent the damn night on her couch. She was certainly fine for a few hours.

He thought back to her saying she slept so much better with him there, and he couldn't for the life of him figure out what to do with the…sense of purpose and satisfaction that gave him.

Simmons offered a wave and started pushing the unwieldy stroller toward him, so Royal walked toward him instead of away. He couldn't resist looking around to see if Daisy Delaney was going to appear.

"My wife isn't here, if that's who you're looking for," Simmons said somewhat irritably when they met on the sidewalk. "Lucy's out of town, so I'm on kid duty and let's just say we all needed some fresh air before we all started crying."

Royal peered into the double stroller. A kid clutched a giant plastic dinosaur and was fast asleep. The baby—the one that had been crying the other day—was sitting there babbling to herself happily. She held a sock in one pudgy hand and was waving her bare foot around like she'd amazed herself at what she was capable of.

For a second, he was struck by the idea that Brooke would have one of these soon enough. It was kind of a nice thought. She'd have a baby to push around in a stroller and who would grow up and run around that big ranch, happy and protected and loved. So unlike everything they'd been given.

But that was the future and this was the present.

"You got anything for me on the woman?"

"I'm still pulling a few old threads, but no one I know and trust at the FBI knows who she is. I can almost guarantee she's not a Fed, but it worries me you thought she was one. When this all started, the sheriff seemed to think you'd have a good eye for that kind of thing."

"Yeah." Royal ignored the speculative look from Simmons, considered this new information. "What about other agencies? Maybe not FBI. Would ATF or someone be involved? You know what Albennie Ward is mixed up with better than I do."

"Yes and no." Simmons shook his head. "I don't want to poke too hard, raise any suspicions, so it's *possible* she could be with a random department, but…"

"It feels off." Royal studied Main Street around them. It was a quiet day. "I have a theory. I can't confirm yet, but someone started a fire with Franny's books in Sunrise this morning. Apparently, yesterday a woman no one knew got a library card at the Sunrise library and checked out all Franny's books."

"A woman… You think it's the same woman."

"It's not the male kidnapper. So… It's a theory. Copeland is running the woman's name, but it'll be fake."

"I guess you could try to get an APB out, or something through Bent County, but…"

Royal could read Simmons's reluctance. "It's delicate. I feel like… This is a case where we don't want to tip anyone off. We need to keep things close to the vest."

Simmons nodded. "Agreed, Deputy."

Which brought him back to the thought he'd been ruminating over all morning. He'd figured if he went through with it, he wouldn't tell anyone, but maybe… Maybe Simmons was the guy to tell. "I—I know someone who might be able to figure out who she is. Under the table. Not exactly…within the law. But they'd be able to do it without anyone knowing. I can't go through the sheriff for this one."

"Does this person know what they're doing?"

"Probably better than you or me."

Simmons was clearly dubious, but he didn't mount any objections. "How much you think they'll charge?"

Royal shook his head. "It'd be a favor. I just… It's the right course of action, don't you think? Find out who this woman is kind of under the radar? If you weren't worried there was some kind of FBI leak, you'd have them do it, wouldn't you?"

Simmons nodded. "I would."

"All right." Royal couldn't help but be a little concerned that by not taking this to the sheriff he was stepping out of his lane, risking his job.

But he couldn't go against his gut instincts that this was right, and the best option to keep Franny safe.

He was distracted momentarily by some grunting and groaning sounds. He looked into the stroller again. The boy was waking up, wriggling and noise making enough to earn his sister's wide-eyed attention.

"Keep me in the loop, Campbell," Simmons said, pushing the stroller forward. "If I have to fall on the grenade, let me know. Sheriff can't fire me."

Royal laughed in spite of himself. "I'll hold you to that."

More roaring from the little boy in the stroller.

"I better get him something from the bakery before he turns into a pint-sized monster."

The boy squealed. "I'm a T-Rex! Not a *monster*."

"Oh boy, here we go," Simmons muttered under his breath. "Let me know, Campbell."

Royal nodded, watched Simmons go for a few seconds, trying to reconcile having that conversation over two cute kids. He shook his head. Well, life was weird.

And about to get weirder, because now he had to figure out how to ask Zeke for a favor.

Chapter Fifteen

Franny didn't leave her apartment. She didn't even leave her bedroom except to eat. The writing wasn't going *quite* as well as it had the other day. As much as she wanted to think about fictional worlds, lose herself there, her brain kept wandering back to book burning.

Her books.

So when the writing couldn't distract her from the creepy, crawly *targeted* feeling, she let herself be distracted by the internet. About the only thing that took her mind off her anxiety was watching videos of a concert she'd never attend. Then she called Audra back—because of course Copeland had run his mouth and told her about Royal being there this morning.

"He just spent the night on the couch because he fell asleep, and I didn't want to wake him up, because he's running himself ragged watching out for me."

"Hmm," was all Audra had said.

"Trust me, Audra. He's like…" She thought about everything he'd told her about the Sons. About foster homes. She was so…pampered and privileged in comparison. There was just no way he saw anything interesting in her. "He's not into me."

"You've never been a very good judge of that."

"I swear, Audra. He's touched me all of three times. And it's that friendly cop-to-victim attagirl pat each time."

"Cataloguing it?"

"Well, sure. He's hot. He has tattoos."

Audra snorted. Luckily for Franny, Audra had a million things to do at the ranch, so she'd been able to move the conversation quickly along, promising to go over to the ranch for dinner once this whole *surveillance* thing was over. She got an update on Rosalie—sick as a dog but finally taking the anti-nausea medication. Then she said goodbye.

And spent the next two hours doomscrolling.

When it got to be close to seven, she forced herself out of bed. She'd make dinner again. Maybe Royal would stop by and she could con him into staying again. Probably not fair. Probably not what she should *try* to do.

But she was just so much more at ease when someone was here. Not just *any* someone, because there were *cameras*. It had to be someone she was comfortable with, and since Audra had ranch business and Rosalie had puking and baby-growing business, and Vi had her ever-growing family to contend with… Royal was just going to have to suck it up.

Or tell her no.

Before she could talk herself out of the sinking feeling in her stomach at the thought of him *refusing* and how embarrassing that would be, her phone chimed.

Coming up.

It was from Royal. She appreciated that he texted first, so her heart didn't jump into her throat in fear at an unexpected knock. But why was he here? Did he *want* to eat dinner with her every night?

"Don't be ridiculous," she muttered, turning off the security system and then going to unlock the door and open it.

He looked just about the same as he had last night, in fresh clothes and wet hair like he'd run through the shower after his shift. There was just *something* that happened inside of her every time she saw him. It wasn't just thinking he was hot—she thought plenty of guys were hot. It was something in the eyes, the serious cast of his mouth pretty much always, even when he laughed.

Because his childhood was the worst, Franny. Not because he's a brooding romance hero.

"Hi." She shifted out of the doorway so he could come in, but he didn't move forward right away.

"Hey. You busy?"

"Oh, no. Just…figuring out what to eat for dinner. Um, I can make enough for two if you want to stay again."

"Actually, I promised my sister I'd have dinner at her place tonight. Something we try to do once a week."

She *refused* to feel disappointed. She *refused* to let her expression fall. She kept her smile bright, but before she could think of what to say like, *please don't.* He kept talking.

"I came over to see if you want to come with."

"Come…with." She had no idea what to do with that invitation or how to feel about it. She wanted to, *obviously*, but this was his sister and… If it was pity, she didn't want his full-blown pity.

Did she?

"Sure. I'm picking up a pizza. And you've already met, right? So, nothing crazy. Just be two hours probably." He shrugged, all casual and at ease while her lungs seemed to tie themselves into a knot.

"Is this because you feel sorry for me, or because you literally think I'm in that much danger?" She wouldn't allow herself to think about any third option, or Audra saying she never recognized when men were into her.

He most assuredly was *not*. This was business. Protection. His *job*.

He studied her for a long drawn-out minute, standing there in her doorway. He had a way of standing that *seemed* casual, but then she caught that intensity in his eyes, and it dispelled her of that notion right quick. But it certainly didn't stop the obnoxious fluttering thing her heart was doing.

"I don't feel sorry for you," he said very carefully. "I don't think you're going to wind up dead if I leave you here, but I have…concerns if I'm out close to Sunrise and you're here. It's just too much space. But Mayfield's a good cop from what I've seen. If you want to stay, I can turn over the surveillance stuff to him until I get back."

She was already shaking her head. "No." Maybe she should be fine with any cop handling her surveillance, but it had set her on edge enough and she knew, trusted, *liked* Royal. She'd never even met this Mayfield. "I'll…go with you." She looked down at her outfit—the same thing she'd put on this morning in a panic. "I need to change first."

"You look fine for pizza."

She waved him in, shaking her head. "You're a man who looks good in whatever you put on. You don't understand."

"You look good," he said closing the door behind him.

She could *not* engage with that. Because if she did…she might read into it. He was just being polite. "No, you said I look *fine*, and I don't. I look like… I've been rotting in bed all day. Because I *have*."

"Does it matter?"

She fisted her hands on her hips and gave him her best

glare. "Do you want to keep arguing or do you just want to let me get dressed?"

He made a waving motion for the hallway. So she went into her room, inwardly groaned that she could not take her time thinking this through. What did you wear for a pizza dinner at your protector cop's sister's house? When you were the sad victim, not an actual guest.

Match Royal's vibe. Casual. Relaxed. She changed out of her yoga pants into jean shorts with a plain blouse—slightly elevated from a T-shirt but not fancy. Then tennis shoes, because if she remembered correctly, Brooke lived on a ranch. Footwear should match the location.

Hair? No mirror. She grabbed a clip off her dresser, twisted her hair up, then used her phone to use the camera as a kind of mirror.

Once she was satisfied—or at least as satisfied she was going to get in a few minutes—she went back out to the main room. Royal was standing in front of her bookcase.

And she was back to thinking about someone purposefully burning all her books.

"You got a favorite?" he asked, pointing at the shelf where she'd arranged her own books.

"Of my books?"

He nodded.

She wasn't sure why he'd ask, but she gave it some thought as she walked over to stand next to him. The physical representation of the past seven years of work. "I don't know that I have a favorite. They all mean…something different, I guess." She reached out, tapped her fourth one. "This one though? Rejected by my first editor, so selling it to a new publisher—and then having it do well—probably the one that brings the biggest smile to my face."

He chuckled. "Spite determines your favorite?"

"Spite is a great motivator."

His mouth curved. "Yeah, I guess it is."

"You're not a police officer out of spite."

"Maybe not, but it didn't hurt thinking about how much my dad would hate it when the academy was annoying as hell. Kinda spitey."

"Kinda," she agreed, amused. More…thrilled than she had any sensible right to be that he understood.

"Well, we better head out," he said. "I promised Brooke I'd pick up the pizza, and she likes to remind me you shouldn't leave a pregnant woman hungry."

"Oh, she's having a baby? Isn't that great?" She grinned at him as they left the apartment. She locked the door and set all the alarms. "Uncle Royal."

"Yeah, I guess." He grunted, leading her down to a car that wasn't his police cruiser. "Kinda weird."

They settled into the car. "I love being an aunt—well, honorary aunt, because I don't have siblings. But I got to help Vi when she had Magnolia, so I became Aunt Franny, though Mags calls me Geen."

"Why?"

"Not a clue, but even now that she's stringing full sentences together, I'm still Geen. It's cute. And then Fox came along, and he's the sweetest little pudge ball. And now Rosalie is having a baby? It's the best. You get to spoil and play and be fun instead of having to worry about keeping a whole other human alive twenty-four-seven."

"Not sure I know how to *be fun* with an infant."

"Oh, it's easy," Franny said waving that away as they drove. "I'm guessing the teenage years will be the hardest, but then you just take them to the R-rated movie their parents don't want them to see or buy them the energy drink their parents won't let them have."

He eyed her. "You're really planning on walking on the wild side."

She laughed, even though he was kind of making fun of her. "Wild is my middle name."

"I just bet," he replied with a grin that had the damn *flutter* taking it up a notch, but he pulled into the pizza parlor parking lot. "I'll be right back." It only took a few minutes before he reappeared with a big box of pizza and a bag balanced on top. He secured the pizza in the back seat, then drove again.

Conversation did not naturally return, and the silence made her nervous, so she figured he was going to have to deal with her annoying questions.

"So, Brooke is married to…somebody from the Hudson family from Sunrise?"

Royal shook his head. "No. Zeke Daniels. His brother and sister are married to Hudsons."

"Right. Okay. And Zeke is a rancher?"

"Yeah. Or trying to be anyway. Him and Brooke seem to like figuring it all out."

She could hear the bafflement in his tone. "No ranching aspirations?"

"Not a one. I had my fill of living out in the great wide open."

"Bent County isn't exactly a thriving metropolis."

"Yeah, I haven't got any interest in that either. I don't want extremes. I want something…straightforward. Besides, I wanted to settle somewhere close to Brooke more than I cared what kind of place that was."

She didn't point out that straightforward was *not* exactly how she'd describe Bent County, because him wanting to be close to his sister was sweet.

He turned off the highway onto a kind of bumpy lane.

In the distance was a house. It was a lot like Audra's. A little…sagging around the edges, age and weather taking their toll, but a lot of effort to make it look like…home, she supposed. Lace curtains in the windows. A porch swing painted a pretty blue. Flowers planted along the base of the porch that popped in colorful summer blooms.

Royal parked his car next to a big truck and got out. Franny followed suit and the front door opened.

A dog came running out, barking up a storm as he rushed over to Royal, tail wriggling in excited pleasure.

Franny froze. It had been so long since she'd been in the kind of situation where she went to someone's house that she didn't know, she'd forgotten to ask.

Royal greeted the dog by crouching down to pet it. He let the dog lick his face while Franny stood out of the way, stock-still. He glanced over at her. Franny could practically see the fur flying through the air and toward her. Her eye almost twitched in anticipation.

"Afraid of dogs?"

"Uh. No. I love them actually, but I'm…fairly allergic."

He narrowed his eyes. "What's *fairly* mean in Franny world? Deathly?"

"I won't…die." She always had her inhaler in her purse. And it wasn't a cat. But she didn't think she had any of her antihistamines with her. She was just so good at managing her exposure, she didn't carry around all the things she needed. Or *had* been good at managing exposure.

Royal straightened, studying her with that expression that was vaguely disapproving, but not in a way that got her back up. She didn't know how to describe it. It was closer to concern than…disapproval.

"Well, it's not too hot out with the sun setting. I'll suggest to Brooke we eat outside. She's got furniture out here on the porch." He got the pizza out of the back, holding it up high so the dog couldn't jump at it. He started moving toward the porch and Franny scurried after him.

"You don't have to do that. I can handle a little dog fur." Maybe. She hadn't had any allergy shots since moving to Wyoming, but what was a few hours? She'd take a pill when she got home, shower off all the fur, and be *fine*. Ish.

"Don't be a martyr, Franny," he told her as he began to stride toward the door where Brooke now stood. She had an arm draped over an adorable baby bump and was smiling in warm welcome.

"You mind if we eat out here on the porch?" Royal said as he approached. "Franny's allergic to dogs."

"Oh, sure. No problem. I'll have Zeke put her inside. Come here, Viola." Brooke patted her thigh and the dog came running.

"Oh, you don't have to—"

At Royal's sharp look, she shut her mouth. "Thank you."

"Good girl," he murmured.

Which should be insulting. Not kinda hot.

DINNER WAS...NICE, ACTUALLY. Not that Royal had expected it to be *bad*, just maybe a little awkward. But Brooke and Franny seemed to have endless topics to discuss. It made it easy to relax a little, and he figured it was good for Franny to get out. Feel normal, even for a few hours.

She could go have a meal with her cousins, but he had a feeling she hadn't asked for that because she knew they would just worry and hound. Dinner out here was like pretending nothing was wrong.

Royal was just biding his time, waiting for a chance to talk to Zeke alone. When Franny asked Brooke about some flower and they got up to go peruse Brooke's gardens, Royal hung back with Zeke. At some point, Brooke took Franny inside to show her something, so Royal finally had the privacy to discuss what he'd come there to discuss with Zeke.

"I've got a favor to ask."

"What kind of favor?"

"A former secret agent who still keeps in contact with all those other former secret agents favor."

"I'm retired." Zeke leaned back in his chair and crossed his arms over his chest. "And I don't help cops."

"Since when?"

Zeke looked him up and down. "Since *you* became one."

Royal snorted in spite of himself. He and Zeke had found a lot of even ground, what with both wanting the best for Brooke, but part of that even ground was giving each other a hard time.

"Will this favor help your…friend?" He jerked a chin toward the door Franny and Brooke had gone in.

"She's not a friend. She's a *witness* I'm protecting." Which felt like a lie. "But yeah, it's to help her."

"All right. Shoot."

Royal filled Zeke in on the suspicious woman in Hope Town—and a few of Royal's theories. "If she's not a Fed, I want her identity. Especially if she started that fire."

"Dahlia was pretty upset about it."

Reminding Royal that everything in Bent County was connected. Because Zeke's siblings were both married to Hudsons—and Dahlia the librarian was married to a Hudson.

"Email me the picture, and your bodycam footage if you can. I should be able to get a look at Dahlia's description myself, but it wouldn't hurt to send it my way if you get a sketch. I'll look into it. If I can't figure it out, I'll send it up the former secret agent chain. We should be able to ID her."

"Thanks." It eased a little of the tension inside of him, though it would no doubt wind back up again if this took too long.

"Just a warning. Brooke's matchmaking."

"Matchmaking what?"

"You and your friend, I mean *witness*. She heard you were bringing a woman, and she immediately started picking out wedding decorations."

Royal scoffed. "Surely she's not that delusional."

"Romantic bliss will do that to you."

"Bliss with you? My ass," Royal grumbled. "Let me know when you figure out who the picture is. I've got to take my *witness* home." He pushed out of his chair at the same time the door opened.

"Royal, I think you better take Franny home," Brooke said, worry written all over her face.

"I'll be fine, really," Franny said, sounding…weird. Kind of squeaky. "I just have to take a shower, an antihistamine, and I'll be—" She sneezed. Twice. "—back to normal."

"You sound *horrible*."

She looked over at him, and he thought maybe she was trying to glare, but…

"And your eye is…swollen or something."

She sneezed again. Her eyes were watering and the swollen one looked like it was…pulsing.

"I'm so sorry, Franny," Brooke said again. She held out a wet washcloth. "Why don't you try to wipe your face again?"

Franny took it, wiped it over her face. "Please don't be sorry." Sneeze. "It's my own…" Sneeze. "…fault. I forgot how bad…" Sneeze. "…it can get, and I should have asked if you had a cat." Sneeze. "I haven't been around any in a while and…" She trailed off and sneezed three times in quick succession.

Royal took her by the arm, tried not to notice his sister's expression going from worry to *notice.*

"Let's get you home," he told Franny.

She held out the washcloth to Brooke, but Brooke refused. "You take it with you. Royal will bring it back. No worries."

He led her down to the car. She sneezed the whole way, sputtering out thanks and goodbyes and apologies as her face turned redder and her eye seemed to get even *more* swollen. He went to the back of his car and grabbed a box of tissues. When he slid into the driver's seat, he handed it to her. "Here."

She shook her head. "I'm allergic to tissues."

"What?"

"It just makes it worse. I have to use handkerchiefs or napkins or paper towels or…" She went into another sneezing fit.

"Why'd you go in the house?" he asked, baffled by this entire thing. He left the ranch, pushing the speed limit more than he usually would.

"Brooke had the book I wrote that she helped with, and she wanted me to autograph it, so I did that." She sneezed. "I *am* terribly allergic to dogs, but it would have been fine. I'm usually fine for a little bit. But there was a cat…" She gestured to her face.

And sneezed, four times in a row. "Cats are worse. Still, it's been a long time and maybe I was a little optimistic I'd grown out of the allergy. You know, they change every seven years."

She said it so earnestly he found himself with twin urges to laugh and just…gather her up and take care of her.

He resisted both. "Do I need to take you to the hospital?"

She shook her head. Sneezing through another sentence. "I just need to get home. Run through the shower, take an allergy pill. I'll be good as new."

She fumbled with her purse, then pulled out a little contraption. Once she put it to her mouth he realized it was some kind of inhaler.

"Franny…"

She took another big breath of air from that thing, still shaking her head. "A shower. That's all."

He was more than a little concerned she needed an entire hospital stay, but he followed her instructions and just drove back to Hope Town while she kept sneezing and wiping her face with the washcloth Brooke had given her.

He pulled up next to her stairway, parked illegally. She got out of his car about as fast as he did, fumbling through her purse again.

"Give me your keys," he muttered.

She handed them over while she fumbled with her phone to turn off the security alarm. She wasn't sneezing quite as much, but she was still red and looked miserable.

Once they were inside, she handed him her phone. "You can set the alarm and leave if you want. I'm going to run through the shower." Then she made a beeline for the hallway.

He looked down at her phone in his hand. He obviously wasn't going to *leave*. He set it on her kitchen counter, then paced the small area.

What could he do? He wanted to…do *something*. Fix it. Hell, it was practically his fault. He'd taken her over to Brooke's. He could have just left her under Mayfield's watch. That's what he *should* have done.

And he could tell himself a lot of reasons why that had been, *had* told himself a lot of reasons. But he knew none of them mattered as much as the non-police one.

He liked being around her. He'd wanted to see her with Brooke. He'd wanted…something he couldn't quite articulate to himself.

Or maybe he could, thanks to Zeke. *Matchmaking.* He scoffed, taking a few steps toward the hallway.

She was pretty and funny and interesting, but what was he? A kid from a biker gang. He'd done terrible things in his life. Maybe mostly for good reasons, or to try to protect people, but… They were still there, living inside of him. His record could be expunged, but his memories couldn't.

And Franny was privileged and…*nice.* She'd probably never had so much as a speeding ticket. She'd gone into that house to sign his sister's book to be nice.

She was kind. Down to the marrow.

And you want a piece of that.

Yeah, maybe he did.

As little as he *should.*

Chapter Sixteen

Franny felt mortified. She tried to let the hot spray of the shower wash away that feeling along with all the allergens.

It didn't work. Well, she stopped sneezing. The throbbing behind her eye was starting to fade. Eventually the antihistamine would kick in. She'd probably be a little tired, but by the morning she'd feel good.

Well not *good,* because the humiliation settled deep.

She'd just wanted to feel *normal*. Instead she'd proven to literally everyone involved she was the opposite. When it had been so nice to leave the apartment, to leave Hope Town, to not worry about library cards or burned books or Albennie.

Brooke was so nice, and Franny kind of missed being on a ranch. Or maybe she just missed it because it had felt like freedom.

On a deep, only *slightly* wheezy breath, she turned off the water. Her eyes had stopped watering, and she hadn't sneezed in a while.

She hadn't grabbed clothes before she'd come in there. Well at least she had a towel or that would be *really* embarrassing if he hadn't left.

Surely he'd left. Hightailed it back to safety. He was

probably talking with Brooke right now about what a strange little weirdo he'd been assigned to protect.

She dried her hair then wrapped the towel around her, just in case. She stepped out of the bathroom then stopped short. Royal was standing there. For a moment, they were both perfectly still, staring at each other.

Then he jerked his head up, looking at the ceiling.

But there was that…brief second where his gaze had drifted…down.

Wasn't there?

"Sorry. I thought you'd…be dressed," he said, sounding gruff. "I just wanted to… Do you need anything? I'm still worried about you."

Worried. That was…sweet. But she was *in a towel*. "All my clothes are in my room. So I'm just going to…" She sidestepped, holding the towel tight. "Get dressed. I'm good. I'll…be out in a minute." She nearly *leaped* for her door and then closed it very firmly behind her.

It was silly. The towel covered what any dress would. Well, maybe not *any* dress as she wasn't prone to wearing anything that short, but still.

It didn't matter. He wasn't looking at her any way, and the *worry* was that the woman he'd been assigned to protect might die from cat allergy instead of crazed kidnapper she'd IDed.

Frustrated with herself on just about every level, she pulled on some baggy athletic shorts, and because she couldn't be bothered to put on a bra, an athletic top with support built in. She left her hair damp and down, because it didn't matter *how* she looked.

He'd seen her use her inhaler. She needed to stop holding on to some strange little seed of hope that the hot cop who'd grown up in a *biker gang* thought there was anything even remotely interesting about her.

She stepped out of her bedroom, determined to play all of this as just *normal*. Something that could happen to *anyone*. Ha. Ha. *Ha*.

But he was standing there still. Right across from her room door. Waiting for her.

She tried to smile but wasn't sure she managed. "All better," she said brightly.

But he crossed the small space between them. He studied her face very intently, then framed her face with his very large, very rough hands and tilted her face up toward the light.

For signs of allergic reaction, Franny. Stop letting your imagination play tricks on you. Because in her imagination this would lead somewhere *very* different. In her imagination, she was the kind of woman who knew how to issue an *invitation*.

And then knew how to behave if such invitation was accepted.

"Are you sure you're okay?" he asked very seriously.

"Yeah." She nodded. He didn't move his hands, so her cheeks just kind of brushed up against the rough palms. *God*. "I'm a big girl. I know how to take care of myself."

He cocked his head.

"Well, you know, with how to handle an allergy attack. Not so much the whole kidnapper threatening me thing." She tried to smile, but he was so *close*. "See? I haven't sneezed once since I got out of the shower."

"Yeah, an improvement, but your eye's still swollen." And then his thumb swept under said eye, and she forgot all about the pounding in her temples, that swollen feeling when she blinked, how much her eyes itched.

Because he was touching her with such gentleness and touching her at *all*. Even though she knew he was doing it in like a first responder, worried about her health way, she couldn't get that message through to all the pleasure receptors in her body.

"Well, uh, the allergy meds will take a little while to kick in. But I already feel ten times better. And learned my lesson that I did not, in fact, grow out of my terrible dog and cat allergy."

She should move her head. Step away. She knew she should, but her body wasn't listening.

And *he* wasn't moving. His hands were still on her face. His expression had changed slightly. He didn't look…concerned.

He looked intent.

Stop. Dreaming.

But she didn't heed the warning in her head. She stayed very still. She was afraid to move. If she moved, he might move. And she wanted to stay right there for as long as humanly possible.

What happened to not imagining things?

But then he was closer. His head tilting toward hers, his hands still on her face. She could feel his breath across her mouth, the warmth of his body. She could smell…something on him. Soap or cologne or…

His mouth was just a whisper away from hers, and she could think of no rational reason for it. Checking her pulse? Making sure her eye hadn't fully swollen shut?

No, none of that made sense, the only thing that made sense…even though it *didn't*, was that he was…going to kiss her.

And he did. Kind of. His lips touched hers. She barely felt the contact. It was so light. Like a test. For both of them.

She'd always enjoyed acing tests, so she moved to her toes, touching her hands to his chest as balance.

And then it wasn't light at all. His grip on her face changed, somehow firming and gentling at the same time. The kiss wasn't…*wild*, but she didn't know what it was. Serious, like him. Intent and thorough and absolutely mind-emptying.

And it just seemed to *last*. He lingered, and she lingered, and surely she was just hallucinating or something, but she'd take it. If it felt this good, she'd sure as hell take it. Especially since she could feel the unsteady beating of his heart under her palm.

He eased away, but for a moment their lips still faintly brushed, their breath a little ragged, mingling. She inhaled deeply, opened her eyes. To his blue ones staring intently at her.

Then he kind of *sighed*, slowly dropping his hands. Then stepping back, leaning against the wall opposite her.

Franny didn't breathe. Her skin *buzzed*. And there was not one useful thought in her head. Not *one*.

He had kissed her, and she could not rationalize that simple fact away.

Royal cleared his throat. "I… I should apologize."

Apologize. Right. *The humiliation continues*. "Okay."

"It's just… I shouldn't be…" At least he seemed *almost* flustered. He wasn't *trying* to humiliate her.

Just succeeding at it.

"You don't have to explain," she said, proud of how… calm her voice sounded. "You didn't like it. You don't have to manage my feelings." She even smiled at him, because he *didn't*. That was her job. And she was damn good at it.

But he didn't move out of the way. He frowned down at

her. "Didn't like… That's not why I'm sorry. It was a good kiss, Franny."

She opened her mouth, but…no, she had absolutely no words ready to respond to that. He'd really emphasized the word *good.*

"But this is my job. My *new* job. Maybe I'm off field training, but I'm still on probation for six months. They can fire me for *no* reason if they want, and I came into the job with reasons, Franny. I don't want to give them another one. If I'd been stupid enough to do that about ten feet to the left, it would have been on *video.* And I'd have been out on my ass."

Well, *that* was a sobering thought.

"I crossed a line. One I can't afford to cross again." He said it so…forcefully. Maybe she hadn't fully realized until right now just how *important* his job was to him. She knew, just from what she picked up on, that getting on the right side of the law meant something to him, but *this* job in particular wasn't something he was going to jeopardize.

She could accept that. It was actually very honorable—though she didn't think he quite saw himself that way. But *she* did. Maybe… Maybe she could find a way to show that to him. Just how far he'd come, if he wasn't willing to accept it himself.

She desperately wanted to do that. He *deserved* that. So she smiled at him. "So, hypothetically, when this is all over…assuming you know, I don't get murdered by some crazed kidnapper in the process, a kiss like that could… repeat itself. Once the job was over?"

ROYAL STILL DIDN'T know what had possessed him. Well, he understood the *inclination*, just not having the control to *stop* the actual *acting* on the inclination.

She just looked… Something about the wet hair and the swollen eye and her smiling at him like she was *fine*, when she was a bit pathetic, it undid something in him.

It shouldn't. It didn't make sense that it did. And yet he couldn't seem to rationalize all these…impulses when it came to her away.

He desperately wanted her to be safe and comfortable and happy and… Boy, if he started inserting himself into her life that was not going to lead to any of those things.

He wanted to say so many things. Mainly that there were no hypotheticals about it. The minute it didn't threaten his job he wanted his mouth on her. Among other things.

But that was the problem.

"I don't think you understand…" He didn't know how to articulate that this was a *him* issue. She seemed so certain… Saying he didn't like the kiss when he'd been the damn one to initiate it. She seemed so sure of herself, but those little uncertainties shone through and just…

She needed someone who… Who was *actually* the guy he pretended to be. *Actually* honorable and dedicated to the law, through and through. Not a screwed-up kid from a biker gang trying to make some kind of weird amends to his sister and maybe himself.

"Franny, I'm not a *good* guy. I've done and seen some… truly awful things."

She studied him with those big green eyes, all soft and considering, like she *understood* him, but not in the way he wanted her to. In some deeper way he didn't fully grasp.

"Royal, I think the fact you've become a police officer, that you want to do good things in the face of all the bad you were surrounded with is something to be proud of. It's brave."

He had no words. *Brave*. He'd mostly called any *brave*

he'd demonstrated survival. Because that's all it really was. Sometimes you had to face fear not because you wanted to, not because you were *brave*, but because you wanted to survive.

Franny had probably never considered *survival* in her life, and he was glad for that. Glad something awful didn't weigh on her. He didn't want it to.

But for a brief, painful moment, he wanted to be as *brave* as she thought he was. Instead of just someone who knew how to survive.

Before he could decide what to do with that, or *this*, his phone rang. He pulled it out of his pocket. The readout was the sheriff's department.

"I better take this," he said, swiping to answer and stepping away from her. "Deputy Campbell."

"Campbell. Sheriff here. I've just gotten a call from one of the FBI agents who was here. They've found Albennie Ward. I don't have the details yet, but they're bringing her back to Bent."

For a moment, Royal was speechless. *Found.* "What about who took her? The kidnapper?" The woman that had been creeping around that the sheriff didn't know about?

"Like I said. No details."

"If we don't know if the kidnapper has been apprehended…"

"You can keep an eye on Ms. Perkins until we have the details. Once I get more information, we'll reevaluate your assignment."

"Yes, sir." He ended the phone call with the sheriff, looked over at Franny.

"They…found her."

"She's okay?" she asked, wide-eyed and hopeful.

"The sheriff doesn't have details just yet, but she's alive

and on her way back to Bent." Relief crossed her features and she kind of sagged there against the wall. He wanted to offer support. An arm to hold her up, a body to lean on.

He stayed where he was, tried to order his thoughts. Tried to think like a *police officer*. Not someone who wanted to make everything okay for Franny.

He could call Simmons and probably get more answers and quicker, but he thought of the stroller and the kids and the late hour. He could wait. They could wait. Sheriff had told him to stay put.

"We don't know who's been arrested, so we continue on tonight just like we've been doing until we know for sure the kidnapper is behind bars."

"Can I tell Lia? I have to tell her. She'll be… God, it'll just take such a weight off."

"We don't have any information. Albennie could be hurt. There could be more to this. I don't want to sound cynical. I just don't want to get anyone's hopes up that everything is great when we don't know that for sure."

Franny nodded along. "But… You're not wrong, Royal, but Albennie's *alive*. Even if it's not all sunshine and roses, she's alive and coming home. Lia needs to know."

He couldn't argue with that. "All right. Just make sure to be clear we don't have any details. There's nothing we can do right now except wait for morning."

"Of course," Franny agreed. She made a move for the living room, but Royal couldn't…just stay there. "I should probably go."

She stopped, slowly turned. "Oh."

He forced himself to move forward. To be a damn police officer. "For now, I still want you following all the same precautions, okay? I don't have enough information to be sure they've got the kidnapper locked up, and we still haven't figured out the identity of that woman." He made a beeline for the front door. "We're still keeping you safe, Franny. Until it's all for sure."

She trailed after him.

"You could stay again." Her smile was a little wobbly. It wasn't an *invitation*, in that sense of the word. It was because she was still worried about her own safety, like she should be.

But he had a bad feeling if he stayed, it could *turn* into an invitation he wouldn't have the sense to refuse. He sent her a kind smile. "I better not." And those big green eyes were a *big* reason why.

"Okay." She was clasping her hands together like she did when she was nervous, but he couldn't stay and manage her nerves. They had surveillance, they had alarms. He was right across the street.

And with that barrier maybe he could talk some sense into himself.

"Security. Locks. Call or text if you need anything."

She nodded, got her phone out of her purse on the counter. She disengaged the alarm and he unlocked the door and stepped out onto the porch. He waited for her to close the door behind him, listened to the locks click into place. He knew she'd set the alarm. She'd take all the precautions she should.

It took more self-talk than it should to force himself to walk down the stairs and across the street. He surveyed the dark street, saw no signs of life except the occasional light from one of the buildings.

In the dark, everything looked more ghost town than quaint small town. The shadows seemed to loom. Everything was eerily quiet. But when he got to his side of the street, looked up at Franny's building, the lights behind the windows shone like a beacon.

A beacon you aren't answering, buddy.

He'd been so sure if he just…tested the waters she would back off. Instead, she'd pressed her mouth to his, her hands on his chest, and upended something inside of him he'd thought too cynical to *ever* be upended.

Maybe he'd blame Brooke and her happiness and her baby bump.

Maybe he'd blame allergies and asthma.

Maybe he'd blame his own damn self for being foolish enough to think there was anything good on the other side of everything he'd been through.

Disgusted with himself, he went up the stairs to his apartment. Once inside, he double-checked all the surveillance equipment just to make sure everything was up and running like it should be. Maybe there was a little niggling *impulse* to see if she was on camera, if she was talking to herself, but he wouldn't do that.

It was crossing a line, and maybe he'd been raised to cross lines, *erase* lines, *destroy* every last line. But he'd left that behind. The fact that the impulse still resided in him was what he'd been trying to get through to Franny.

And she'd called him *brave*.

Why did that hit him like a *blow*? Like when Brooke said horribly insightful things about…building a life that the Sons never got to touch. Even if all those scars existed inside them still. Always.

He pulled out his phone, pulled up Franny's contact information and clicked Message. He studied the empty box for a few minutes before he typed up what was on his mind.

Hypothetically, I didn't stay because I don't trust myself

around you. He considered the text for a good ten minutes. Let it sit there without sending. It wasn't *smart* to send it.

But she had *hypothetically* been talking about an after. He should nip that in the bud. Instead he was acknowledging it?

She'd thought he didn't like the *kiss*. He still couldn't get over it. She was so damn pretty and funny and *sweet*, but she didn't necessarily see it. Not enough to think *he* might see it.

He hit Send on the damn text. Then stomped around his apartment, irritated and frustrated, getting ready for bed. He was going to sleep and sleep well. Tomorrow he'd have answers and…

And maybe an *after* to think about, but until then, it didn't matter.

He turned off all his lights, got into bed, then lay there staring at the ceiling.

She tasted like *spring* was all he could think. That sharp, bright slice of hope after a long, dark winter. And he shouldn't think or feel or accept that.

His phone dinged, and he all but lunged for it, figuring Franny would have responded.

But it wasn't Franny. It was a text from Zeke.

We've got a problem.

Chapter Seventeen

Albennie was safe, but even after Franny spoke to Lia, and even though she was exhausted from the allergy attack, Franny still didn't sleep.

Not because she was afraid. Not because her allergic reaction hadn't fully gone away. She didn't sleep because she was *obsessing.*

About that kiss.

About Royal Campbell.

About what was *next* if Albennie was safe and sound in one piece and coming *home.*

It was a relief, but there was such a lack of answers, it was hard to relax and just...believe everything was going to be okay. She had expected Lia to be ecstatic when Franny had called with the news, but she'd been...reserved. Kind of like Royal. Like they were afraid to hope for the best.

It reminded her that Lia had made a joke about hating cops. Maybe it wasn't a joke. Maybe she had a background like Royal did.

Royal.

Her phone pinged. She felt twin pangs of worry and excitement when she saw it was a text from Royal. She opened the text, then just...stared.

Hypothetically, I didn't stay because I don't trust myself around you.

She stared at that text, her heart fluttering in her throat. Didn't *trust* himself around her?

She might actually for the first time in her life understand the word *swoon*. Maybe she shouldn't find that sweet. And hot. And romantic.

But she did.

Except she didn't have the first clue how to respond. She wanted to say something flirty, but she didn't have any experience being that. So she lay there in bed, agonizing over how to respond, but it seemed in only a blink she woke up to the sun streaming through her windows, the phone cradled to her chest.

She'd forgotten to shut the blinds yesterday. And clearly the allergy meds had conked her out, because she'd never responded to Royal's text and it was morning. Late morning at that.

"Way to go, Franny," she muttered, but she didn't even have time to consider self-recriminations because she realized someone was knocking on her door.

And when she looked at her phone screen to see what time it was, she saw she had three new texts from Royal.

I'm giving it two more minutes then I'm breaking down the door, came the last one.

She jumped out of bed, hurriedly typing as she moved for the front door. Because she was pretty sure he would do just that, and even though she was *tempted* to want to see it, she knew she'd feel foolish later.

I'm awake, she texted, then opened the alarm app on her phone and disengaged it. Then she unlocked the front door to Royal standing there, scowling.

He had a to-go cup of coffee in one hand and held it out to her. "Thank you for scaring five years off my life."

She took the coffee he offered her. "I… I'm sorry. I'm a little out of it. The allergy pill really knocked me out last night."

"Lucky," he muttered. He didn't look at her. He surveyed the room. Continuing to speak before she could parse the *lucky*. "The sheriff wants us both to come into the station this morning."

It was so silly to want to just…put her mouth to his and see what he would do. Which was definitely a pre-coffee, post–allergy pill thought. Not a sane one in response to what he'd just said.

"Why?"

"I assume to go over what the FBI have told him about Albennie's return. And what that means for your surveillance and so on."

"Oh, right." Important stuff. Not kissing stuff.

"You might want to get dressed. And brush your hair."

Her free hand flew up to her hair. She could *feel* the rat's nest at the back of her head. Usually she slept like the dead after an allergy pill. Apparently last night she'd slept like the restless dead. And since her hair had still been damp from the shower, it was no doubt a hopeless mess.

His mouth curved, for the first time a spark of something behind the cop facade. "I mean, it's a real cute look and all, but it looks like you've been up to something."

She could feel her cheeks *heat*. She wished she was the kind of woman who had the guts to say something like *I wish we'd been up to something.* But she wasn't Rosalie.

She was just tongue-tied.

"Go on and get ready, Franny," he said, very gently, but his mouth was still curved. Amused at her in a way that never felt condescending.

She nodded and went for her room, because this was important police business stuff.

Then she remembered his text last night.

Didn't *trust* himself.

She blew out a breath. Well, she was just going to have to concern herself with both. She had to contain multitudes.

She tried to find a suitable outfit for the police station quickly so she wasn't leaving Royal waiting, but her mind kept wandering because he'd sent that text and he'd…

He liked her. He was interested in her. It wasn't imagination or wishful thinking. He'd *kissed* her. She hadn't forced him to do that. And he didn't strike her as someone who… would go against his own truth to soothe someone else. He *was* a soother, but it was like…honest soothing.

She shook her head, pulled on some jeans since the police station was freezing. A T-shirt, a jacket she tied around her waist. Her hair was hopeless, but she tried to detangle it a little bit before using a rubber band to create a messy bun that looked purposeful instead of wild.

Then she grabbed the cup of coffee and guzzled down as much as she could.

A latte. Because he knew what she drank. Because he liked her. Didn't trust himself around her. And maybe there was a hope that could all mean something, but they had to step over this whole *kidnapping* business first.

And it was about to be over. It had to be, right? Albennie was coming home. The surveillance would be over. And maybe she and Royal could…go out on a date or something.

Because he *liked* her, and whether that worked out or not wasn't important in this moment. What was important in this moment was not talking herself out of what he'd made perfectly clear.

That and going to the police station.

She went back out into the main part of the apartment.

Royal stood at her window, looking down over Main Street, but he turned when she came in.

For a moment, neither of them said anything. They just stared at each other. And she hoped he was reliving that kiss at least a *little*, because that's where her brain had gone.

"There are things you should know about me, Franny. Things that would change the way you look at me."

He was so serious. Even more serious than his usual. Her heart tripped over itself, but when she spoke her voice was calm. Even if her heart wasn't. "Do I look at you a particular way?"

"Yeah, you do. Like you think I'm good or brave. I'm not."

She wanted to argue with him, but he said it with such *conviction*. So she had no words, just an ache in her heart. Because he could tell her a million things, but she didn't think he'd ever be able to convince her he wasn't good or brave. No matter what he said.

"I've been to jail."

Well, she hadn't expected *that*. But it didn't add up. Not yet. "Then how did you become a police officer?"

"My record was cleared. It was…gang stuff, a frame job. But there were things I did in that gang. I broke the law. I hurt people."

"Because you liked it or to protect people who weren't as strong as you?"

He didn't answer that right away. She hadn't thought he would. She wasn't surprised that he didn't really answer the question at all. Just side-stepped it.

"I belonged there."

She shook her head. She knew she was in out of her depth here. She could never imagine what it was like to grow up with all that awful around you. It broke her heart that some people had to.

But more, it amazed her the strength of spirit to walk out of it. He didn't see that, and maybe she couldn't convince him of it.

But God she had to try. And not just because she wanted some…chance to see where that kiss would go. But because he deserved to see himself as he was.

"If your record was cleared, that makes it sound like you didn't. And the law itself didn't think you did. And the entire Bent County Sheriff's Department certainly doesn't think you did either."

"What I did? None of it was heroic."

She tried to really put herself in his shoes. Understand how he might view it. But she couldn't get past the fact…too many people loved him, trusted him. He'd been given too many chances not to be the man he seemed like he was. "Wasn't it?"

ROYAL DIDN'T KNOW why they were having this conversation. She'd just looked at him and he'd seen…too much in her eyes. Hope and care and just what he'd told her—she looked at him and he felt as brave and good as she saw him.

But he wasn't, and she had to know. With that kiss rattling around in his head acting like some kind of…precursor to a bigger change than he'd counted on, he had to make sure she *knew*.

Before they took one more step forward. She had to understand. She could not look at him and see him as her hero.

He had failed too many times to be anyone's hero, and the thought of failing *her* in this moment, in any moment, it hurt too much to bear. It was bad enough when it was Brooke, but Brooke was his sister, his blood. She was stuck with him, with that belief in what he could be.

Franny didn't need to be mixed up with or chained to… all the bad he was. Deep inside.

But Franny crossed the space between them. She stopped only when they were practically toe to toe. She met his gaze, her green one serious and kind. Her hand came up to his bicep.

She could be so awkward and unsure of herself, but the way she saw people was so astute. She'd had him pegged before he'd really told her anything about himself.

So maybe you could listen to her.

But it just felt wrong. Bone-deep wrong. To let anyone think he was anything better than what he was.

"The tattoo you have right here," she said quietly, intently, squeezing his bicep. "When you're wearing a T-shirt, I can only see the bottom of it. But it looks like the bottom of a heart."

He didn't know where she was going with this, or maybe worse, he was afraid he knew exactly where she was going. Because she just seemed to be able to see through him, read him, and it should feel wrong. It *was* wrong.

But he didn't move.

"What is it?" she asked.

He didn't want to tell her, but that would make this line of questioning a bigger deal than it was. "Yeah, it's a heart."

"For what?"

"They don't all have meaning." These days, some just served as a reminder of who he'd been, what he'd allowed, all he'd failed.

"For what, Royal?" she repeated, very calm but the kind of calm he could recognize wasn't going to falter or be pushed away. He had to tell her. Somehow...she'd know if he lied.

"The people I couldn't save." It came out on a rasp. A secret he'd never told anyone. That heart on his bicep. A reminder that he could make himself stronger and strong and stronger.

But it'd never save those girls in the gang he hadn't been able to get out.

"Do you have a tattoo for all the ones you did save?" she asked in that same gentle tone. But she knew.

He didn't know how, but he knew she did.

He couldn't speak. Even if he'd had any words, his throat was locked shut. This was…too much, too big, and he had to get her to the police station. He had to…

"I'll never be able to imagine what you've been through, Royal. I would… I would be more than happy to listen if you ever wanted to talk about it. But nothing you could say is going to change what I've seen, what I know. Anything you did to survive the horror you grew up in was brave. Anything you feel like you failed at wasn't *your* failure."

He knew that. Brooke had tried to impress that upon him over the years. And he blamed everything on the evil men who'd hurt him and all the people around him. But it didn't bring back the people who'd been lost.

Nothing did. If he'd been stronger though…

"You chose this," she said, tapping his uniform. So earnest. So sure. "You worked for it. You earned that badge and now you wear it with pride. So you can stand there and tell me a lot of things—you can tell me I'll never understand, you can tell me you *feel* like you failed, but you cannot tell me you aren't good or brave, because that is the *heart* of who you are. Period."

Everything in his chest *hurt*. Like he was being cracked open. Worse, that her eyes were shiny like she might cry. Like she meant all this and it meant something to her.

He meant something to her.

"We should go," he managed to grind out, sounding gruff and pained to his own ears.

She sighed, blinked a few times, then nodded.

Chapter Eighteen

When he moved for the door, Franny followed, not trusting her voice. She didn't know what to do with that entire conversation. It was so deep, so profound, and yet…

She hadn't gotten through to him. Did that make *her* a failure?

She did everything she needed to do to secure her apartment, and hoped it was the last time she had to go through that rigmarole.

She climbed into his police cruiser. She didn't dare look at him, because she wasn't going to lose the battle with tears. She wasn't going to look desperate. Not when she was *right*.

They hadn't driven far when Royal's phone rang through the car's Bluetooth system. Since it was connected, she could see the caller ID pop up on the screen of the car. Zach Simmons. "Why is Mr. Simmons calling you?" Franny wondered aloud.

Royal didn't say anything at first. When he spoke, it was very…detached. And she didn't think it was *all* to do with their conversation at her apartment. "I'll call him back."

Which wasn't an *answer*. It was an evasion.

But then her own phone chimed, a text from Audra in

the family group chat about Copeland saying Albennie was saved and demanding to know why Franny hadn't told them.

So Franny had to craft a quick, breezy text about her allergy pill knocking her out the night before and how she was on her way to the sheriff's department to get an update now. Once she was satisfied and hit Send, she realized the car had come to a stop.

She looked up at the police station. Then over at Royal. He was already getting out of the car, so she followed suit. He didn't offer anything as they walked up to the building. No words of support. No encouragements.

Because she'd had to open her big mouth and tell him he was brave and good. Well, she wasn't going to feel bad about that. She *refused*.

When they stepped inside, Copeland was waiting there, which had a little pit of worry forming in her gut. He didn't look happy or relieved. He had that detective stoicism going on.

"Is everything okay?"

Copeland looked from her to Royal. "Let's go hear what the sheriff has to say and find out."

THIS WAS THE last place Royal wanted to be right now. He needed to talk to Simmons about the information Zeke had given him, and what that meant for…everything, but he supposed Albennie being found would trump his own investigation.

Unless…

He didn't let himself think about the unless. Not yet. He put that away like he put away the conversation with Franny. He stood stiff and still and listened to the sheriff.

"Ms. Ward has some minor injuries. While they took care of those in Idaho, she requested her own doctor to check her out on arrival, so no one local has had a chance to talk to her yet. The Feds will share their *public* reports with us, but they're being closemouthed about the entirety of the case."

"So you don't know who did it?" Franny asked. She was the only one sitting. The sheriff had offered her his chair. So it was an odd tableau—sheriff, deputy, detective standing in front of her like she was the boss.

She was looking a little wide-eyed and concerned to be the boss. *Beautiful though.*

A very unhelpful thought.

"*I* don't, but the FBI do. I suppose that's going to have to be good enough."

"With all due respect, sir, it isn't."

The sheriff sent him a sideways glance. Royal should have taken it as censure, but he couldn't help himself.

"Until we have confirmation that the kidnapper Franny witnessed has been arrested, there is still a chance she's in danger even if Ms. Ward isn't."

"I think that's highly unlikely, Deputy Campbell."

"I don't," Beckett said. "I think he's spot-on. Look, we were all operating under the theory the kidnapper was hired muscle. Even if he doesn't connect to Ms. Ward's disappearance in a full-blown way, that means Franny being able to identify and implicate him in a crime is *still* a risk."

The sheriff shifted uncomfortably. He looked from Beckett to Royal to Franny. He smiled at her. Thinly. "Ms. Perkins, would you mind waiting outside for a few moments?"

Franny's gaze moved to his. For a moment that felt too much like that moment in her living room, their gazes just held. Like they could have full-on conversations without speaking.

But they *couldn't*. So Royal gave her a little go-ahead nod. The sheriff would speak more freely if she wasn't there, and he and Beckett could too.

Because this wasn't over for Franny just yet. And no matter what she thought of him, no matter what she'd said this morning, he was going to be right there making sure she was safe. He wasn't failing her, no matter how much it messed with his head.

"Maybe Albennie will tell us," Franny offered as she got out of the seat. "What's going on. Who the kidnapper was. Maybe we don't have to wait for the FBI to."

The sheriff smiled at her. "Maybe." But then he waited for her to leave, and he closed the door behind her.

Royal stood feeling pulled in way too many directions. The conversation he'd had with Zeke last night about the identity of the woman weighed on him. Because it wasn't something he could bring up to the sheriff. It was under the table stuff that could get him fired.

Just like kissing Franny.

He wanted to talk to Simmons about the woman's identity—a former FBI agent was *definitely* a problem as Zeke had said. Instead he had to convince the sheriff that Franny wasn't safe until they had absolutes. And that irritated the hell out of him.

"Sheriff, Franny's own recount of the kidnapping was that Ms. Ward had a hood secured over her head. It's possible she never saw her attacker. It's possible Franny remains the only witness that can pin this on him, *especially* if he was hired muscle and not connected with the group the FBI may or may not have apprehended. With the threats that have been leveled against her, that's a problem."

"And a crime," Beckett tacked on. "Harassment and

threats are a crime. One that happened in our county and we have an obligation to solve."

"That you can continue to investigate, Detective. But we can't surveil her indefinitely," the sheriff replied with a kind of calm detachment that grated against Royal's nerves. "And until there's another threat on Ms. Perkins *after* Ms. Ward's return, I don't see how I can justify it. If she still feels unsafe, she can hire her own security. But our responsibility only goes so far."

"I think it should go at least as far as ascertaining who has been arrested for what."

The sheriff stared him down, and Royal couldn't help but have some concerns that *I kissed the witness and have definitely gotten too deep* was written all over his face.

"You know he's right, Sheriff," Beckett insisted, and Royal was glad for some backup here, even if it came from a personal attachment of Beckett's own.

"At the very least, I'd like to request maintaining the Hope Town assignment," Royal said. "Until we know everything for sure."

The sheriff looked from him to Beckett. Then sighed. "*If* the kidnapper is still on the loose, and that's confirmed by the FBI, I can give you a week to continue the Hope Town assignment, along with Mayfield on nights. But if it goes beyond that, I can't afford it."

The sheriff's assistant poked her head in the door. "Sorry, gentlemen. Sheriff, that FBI agent is waiting for you in the conference room."

The sheriff's scowl deepened. "All right. I'm headed that way, Miranda. You two are dismissed," he said, striding out of the room.

Royal didn't follow right away. He needed to get a grip

on himself before he dealt with Franny. In so many different ways.

"Maybe she *should* get private security," Beckett muttered, still standing next to Royal.

Royal knew the irritation was with the sheriff, but he didn't like the suggestion either way. "She trusts me." She shouldn't but she *did*. So he'd be what she needed him to be, even if he couldn't change all those past parts of himself.

Beckett made a considering type of noise.

Royal sent him a sidelong glance. "What?" he demanded.

Beckett shrugged. "If you've got a personal stake in this, Campbell, it'd set my mind at ease. And my fiancée's."

Royal looked back at the door. "I don't know what that means."

"Yeah, you do."

Maybe he did. But he wasn't about to address it with Beckett. So he moved for the door, but he couldn't *quite* help himself. "Nothing's happening to Franny on my watch."

Chapter Nineteen

Franny sat making small talk with the sheriff's administrative assistant in between the phone calls she fielded. She watched the sheriff leave at Miranda's insistence, then waited for Royal and Copeland to follow.

It took them a few minutes, which made her uneasy. But she fixed a smile on her face when they finally came out. Royal looked irritated. Copeland looked a little smug—which she supposed meant he'd been poking at Royal.

"I'm going to work on getting to the bottom of the FBI stuff," Copeland told her. "Whether they want to tell us or not, we deserve to know. You deserve to know. The sheriff will be diplomatic. I don't have to be."

"Well, don't get fired or anything. You'd drive Audra crazy being around all the time."

"Ha," he replied sarcastically. "Let Royal take you back to Hope Town. Keep locked up with the security. Maybe get some work done. Let us handle it."

Franny nodded. Not because she was going to *let* anyone do anything, but because arguing with a brick wall was pointless.

So she followed Royal back out to the parking lot. He wasn't saying anything. He was clearly thinking, or planning. She could tell from the expression on his face he'd put earlier into some kind of box and shoved it deep down underneath what needed to be done.

"I could talk to Lia," Franny suggested when they were in the car driving back to Hope Town. "Maybe Albennie has told her or she even knows. Maybe she'll tell me now that Albennie's safe."

"Maybe," Royal agreed, still deep in thought as he drove. "Maybe that's not a bad backup plan."

"Backup?"

"Yeah, my plan first. We're not going back to your apartment just yet."

"We're not?" She was more than a little shocked he wasn't bustling her away.

"We're going to Simmons's house."

"Why?"

He sent her a sidelong look. "Because Simmons and I had a discussion about the woman Lia and I saw poking around Hope Town after the kidnapping. And I took the information to someone who has some…skills at finding out who people are."

Franny considered that sentence. What he was saying. What he wasn't. She was pretty sure the only time he'd left Hope Town, or talked to anyone not directly in Hope Town or connected to the police department was when they'd gone to dinner at his sister's ranch last night.

It was natural to extrapolate from there. "Zeke."

He frowned, sent her a quick glance. "How did you know that?"

"Well, I didn't *know*. I guessed. You likely could have missed dinner with your sister, but instead you took me with you. So you could talk to him when Brooke was distracted. Besides, there's something about Zeke that makes it…easy to believe he'd have said skills. It explains last night better than…anything else."

"I don't need Brooke to be distracted. He probably told her about it anyway. I invited you because I didn't like the idea of being that far away if something happened, like I said."

Franny didn't say anything to that. She felt petulant and weird. Uncomfortable and…maybe she'd blame the allergy med hangover on not quite knowing how to navigate *all* of this.

"Brooke likes you," he said, out of nowhere. In a careful way that didn't quite make sense.

"I like Brooke. And Zeke. I even like their animals, even if their cat inadvertently tried to kill me. They've got a sweet little ranch, and you can tell they're…happy together. Settled. It's like my cousins. It's nice watching people build things."

Build. She sighed in spite of herself. She'd watched her cousins and friends *build*, and she felt the exact same as the day she'd moved to Wyoming three years ago.

Until Royal Campbell had kissed her last night. Which was a wild leap, but all *chances* started with tiny seeds. Maybe they didn't all grow, but they all had a *chance*.

He just had to get past…his whole traumatic childhood. *Sure, Franny, why shouldn't he do that just because you told him to?*

"My point is… If you were annoying or whatever, I'd hardly cart you around or stick by your side." He didn't say it begrudgingly exactly, but he was frowning while he said it.

Maybe that's why she said what she did. "You didn't last night."

He flicked her another dark blue glance. "I told you why."

"I think there's a compliment in there?"

Royal blew out an irritated breath. With her? The situation? Both? She didn't know, but he kept talking.

"The point is, Zeke found this woman's identity. She *used* to be an FBI agent. Briefly. I want that to mean that she's only connected to Albennie Ward."

"But?"

"Look, library card catalogue card and burning books? It just doesn't strike me as the kind of threat you get from hired muscle. And we know a woman was involved with checking the books out of the Sunrise library. I want it to be a coincidence, but until I know for sure it is, I'm worried you're not out of the clear. If they didn't catch these people, then the kidnapper, and maybe this woman, knows you can still implicate them. You're a liability to them."

She *really* didn't like that. Unfortunately, she agreed. She desperately wanted it to be over, but it wouldn't be until the person she'd identified was behind bars. And if this woman was connected to him…yeah, her too.

Royal drove through Hope Town, not stopping at their apartments. He drove on out to the outskirts of town, where some of the big showpiece houses were.

When he pulled through a big wrought iron gate, Franny leaned forward in her seat.

"Wow." Franny stared at the house. It shouldn't surprise her considering Mr. Simmons's wife was a famous country singer, whose father had been a famous country singer. That meant money. But…

It was a beautiful old house, with all sorts of interesting features—architecture and windows and a huge wrap-around porch. Landscaping and hanging baskets of blooms complemented everything.

Royal came to a stop in the driveway. For a moment, they both just sat and took in the house.

"And I thought him affording a whole damn town was something," Royal muttered.

Franny chuckled in spite of herself, glancing over at him. His mouth quirked into an amused smile as their gazes caught.

She sighed. Now wasn't the time, but… "Royal…"

"Come on," he muttered. He got out of the car so Franny followed. Not the time.

She could hear the squawk of chickens and noted there was a little coop off to the side toward the back. It was painted red and looked as cute as any Pinterest page.

"It's gorgeous. This would be the perfect place to set a murder." At Royal's sharp look, she smiled sheepishly. "I meant fictionally."

He shook his head and moved up the porch steps, rapping on the door.

Mr. Simmons opened it, a baby on his hip. The image made Franny smile, just like every time she saw Thomas carting around his and Vi's brood. There was just something really nice about watching a man be a good father. Which made her think of Rosalie and Duncan. They'd make such cute babies.

"Thanks for meeting me here," Mr. Simmons said, over the sounds of explosions and dinosaur roaring in the background. He bounced the baby on his hip. "Lucy's supposed to get back today, but I'm solo parenting until she gets home. This whole county is crawling with family, and do you think a one of them could spare some babysitter duties? No. Why? Because we all have too many damn kids."

He led them into a big living room. For as gorgeous and formal as the outside looked, inside was warm and cozy and covered in kid paraphernalia. On a huge screen, *Jurassic Park* was playing.

A little boy was hanging off the arm of the big couch, his eyes on the TV, but he glanced over at them briefly.

"I'm not scared." The boy's eyes were wide and serious. He didn't *look* scared, but the statement spoke of concern.

"Wow. You must be brave like your daddy," Franny offered.

The boy flashed a grin, then his gaze went back to the movie.

"I keep waiting for him to grow out of the dino phase. Hasn't happened yet. Look, I've got some things in my office I'd like to show you, Royal, but…"

"I can take her. Watch him," Franny offered, holding her arms out for the baby. "I'm the aunt babysitter in my family. Lots of practice." Besides, kids were simple. They didn't make her heart ache like Royal's serious blue eyes did.

"Well, she's kind of particular," Mr. Simmons said, but he handed the baby over. Then he watched the baby, who looked up at Franny with serious eyes like her father. But she didn't express negative feelings.

"Huh," Mr. Simmons said.

Franny smiled at him, made a face at the baby. "I'm a natural. I'll keep an eye on things here. You go show Royal whatever you need to."

Mr. Simmons waited a few more seconds, watching the baby for signs of distress, then shrugged. "All right, Campbell. Follow me."

ROYAL WAS *NOT* weirded out by Franny holding a baby. That off feeling in his gut, like when Brooke talked about her own baby plans and futures and families, was a product of spending an entire childhood not being able to trust the future.

It wasn't about *babies*, in particular, it was just like this looming future. That he somehow had to believe in and yet struggled to get past the idea that death or evil was always just waiting in the wings to destroy any kind of happiness or real life.

That his failures meant...whatever waited him on the other side of the Sons wasn't anything *good*.

Except the Sons were gone, and he was a *cop*, and maybe he had to take Brooke's example and start building on... faith.

Franny had tapped his badge and told him he'd earned it. Had he?

Thinking about it left an uncomfortable tightness in his chest, and an itch behind his shoulder blades he couldn't reach. He was almost grateful he didn't have the time to parse it.

Simmons led him into a big office-type room and Royal was glad to have work to focus on over homey living rooms and cute kids.

And pretty brunettes with big green eyes.

Royal relayed the information Zeke had found to Simmons. "This woman's real name is Holand Meyer. She's got a few aliases, but Zeke couldn't connect any of them to Wyoming over the past month. She was an FBI agent stationed in Michigan for about six months five years ago, and then she disappears, more or less. He can make the connection to the aliases, but not much else. He'll keep digging, but the FBI connection is a problem."

"Yeah, it is." Simmons tapped his fingers on his desk. He had at least three computers, and all looked far more complicated than Royal could ever hope to understand. "There's got to be a leak somewhere. Someone who knows about Hope Town in the FBI knows Holand Meyer and fed her that information. Purposefully or not."

"I agree."

"But what's the connection? What connects a kidnapper, a former FBI agent and Albennie Ward?"

"You know," Royal said, tired of people beating around the bush. "Maybe you don't fully know, but you know what Albennie Ward is mixed up in. Or was. You have enough information from your FBI contacts and whatever you do for these women when they come to Hope Town. She's back. She's safe. Now we need to make sure Franny is safe before the sheriff pulls the entire police department. I've got a damn week."

Simmons studied him intently for a few seconds. "You know, I was skeptical about some rookie cop handling this, but I agreed because I figured I could push him around if he was bad at his job."

Royal said nothing. He'd swallow a lot for a chance to succeed at this job, but he'd be damned if he was going to be pushed around by some ex–FBI agent when it came to keeping Franny safe.

"You're not bad at your job, Campbell. I can't disclose Albennie Ward's case, for a lot of reasons. But now that I've got a name, I can look through what I know about it and see if there's any connection to Holand Meyer."

"All right." It wasn't much, but it was better than nothing. "And you'll send me the list of people arrested if you get it before the sheriff's department?"

"Right away." Simmons studied him. "What are your next steps?"

"I don't know. Wait I guess."

"You any good at waiting?" Simmons asked.

Royal thought about the time he'd spent back in the Sons. The things he'd seen and done with an end goal of protecting some of those girls. Any of those girls. He'd had to bide his time back then, too, and play a hell of a lot of games.

"Yeah, I'm a damn expert at waiting," he muttered, turning away from Simmons and walking back out to where they'd come from.

When they got back into the living room, the boy was lying across Franny's lap, still watching the movie intently, but he had one hand gripped on Franny's arm. The baby was sitting next to them, and Franny was dangling a little bird toy in front of her, making her gurgle with laughter.

"She literally doesn't like anyone but me right now," Simmons said, clearly baffled.

Franny looked up at them, a relaxed smile on her face that hadn't been there in days. "I have been called the baby whisperer a time or two."

She carefully disentangled herself from the boy, then lifted the girl and handed her off to Simmons.

Simmons studied her curiously. "You looking for a babysitting job?"

Franny laughed. "Sure, now and then. You've got my number."

He walked them out into the bright light of morning. Franny said cheerful goodbyes to both kids, but with every step toward his cruiser he watched the tension creep back into her shoulders.

"So?" she asked as they climbed into the car.

He wished he had a better answer for her. "Leads, I guess, but not answers."

Franny blew out a breath. "Well, leads are better than nothing."

He slid a glance at her before returning his eyes to the road. She was trying to be positive. She was always trying so hard to…make everything okay for anyone in her orbit.

Case in point, when he parked next to her building rather than his, she turned that warm smile on him. “You don’t have to walk me up.”

He didn’t. The cameras and alarms were all in place, but he went up just the same. Something about the whole day just felt *off.* Was it him? Her? This…*thing* about her that seemed to jumble up his previously held certainty? All those things she’d said to him…

It didn’t matter. He wasn’t letting her out of his sight until he had some answers. He walked up the stairs with her. “Have you had breakfast? We could go down to the bakery and—”

That off feeling finally had a place to land. He grabbed her arm before she could reach forward and put her key in the lock. “Don’t open the door.”

Chapter Twenty

Franny stopped on a dime. Royal's expression was so serious her heart had leaped to her throat. And his grip on her arm was tight. This was an order, through and through.

Danger.

He was frowning at the door as he studied it, keeping his grip on her even though she'd immediately stopped her forward progress.

"See here," he said, pointing to the frame around the latch with his free hand. "That splintering wasn't there before. I studied this lock the first time someone tried to break in. This wasn't here."

She noticed the crack in the door frame now that he pointed it out, but she wasn't sure it hadn't been there before. She'd never paid much attention to the door frame. "Are you sure?" She glanced up at him.

He was sure.

He took her by the elbow, cop gaze moving around as if assessing a threat in every air molecule. "Come on." He led her down the stairs, then across the street, then up the stairs to presumably his apartment.

"What do you think..." But the question died before she could get it out. She wasn't sure she wanted to know what he thought. The idea of someone getting into her apartment was scary enough, but trying to look like they *hadn't* been in there?

Definitely worse.

They made it to his door, but he didn't immediately unlock it. He studied that too.

He shook his head. "Someone's been in here too. Trying to break in or succeeding." He turned in a slow circle on the landing. His gaze zeroed in on something at the bottom of the door. He released her enough to crouch, study it.

"What is it?"

When he didn't speak, her heart started to thud harder, because to her it looked like a smear of…blood. She swallowed. Why would there be a smear of blood going *into* his apartment?

"Royal?"

He stood slowly. He didn't seem at all panicked, even though that's what was starting to hammer in her chest. His blue gaze was intense, but she didn't see even one ripple of fear in it.

"I'm going to take you to… I'll take you to Simmons. He's got that big-ass house. He can keep you hidden away." He'd already grabbed her again and was pulling her back down the stairs.

She jerked her arm away halfway down the stairs. "No."

He looked up at her from where he stood a few stairs down. "Franny, I'm not sure what's going on. I need to get you somewhere safe. This isn't safe anymore."

"If this is dangerous, and it sure as hell seems dangerous if that was *blood*, I'm not going near anyone's *kids*."

"Okay, fair." He shoved a hand through his hair, the first sign this was more than a simple decision for him. "What about your cousin's ranch?"

She didn't really want to pull Audra into the middle

of this either, but Audra *did* know how to shoot a gun. If they were in danger, Audra could at least defend herself. It felt safer than going to Mr. Simmons with his adorable kids around.

"If we're to our last resort," Franny said very carefully, wishing she could come up with something else. "We can go to my cousin's ranch." Blood did feel kind of…last resort. A very bad last resort.

"We might just be getting there." He was back to pulling her along. She could certainly follow him without the hand on her arm, but it was a kind of nice having some kind of anchor.

He wouldn't like that either, would he? Him being her anchor. He wouldn't trust it. But right now, in the midst of danger, neither one of them had the time to consider that.

"What do you think is happening, Royal?" she asked him once they were in his car—his personal one, not his cruiser. He was still in his uniform though. He was still a *cop*, but she knew taking this car meant he was acting as Royal Campbell, not anyone's deputy.

His expression was grim. "I'm not sure, but nothing good, Franny. Nothing good at all. Someone broke into your apartment and mine, bypassing all security systems. There's blood on my stoop. I have a bad feeling if we'd gone in there, we'd have found…worse."

"We need to tell Mr. Simmons. It's his security system. You don't think he…"

"No, I don't think he's got anything to do with this. Not on purpose anyway. You're right. We need to tell Simmons. And Beckett. Someone was in our apartments for a reason, and I can't imagine it was a good one."

"You drive. I'll handle telling them."

He flicked her a glance, then nodded. "Text. That way they can't try to argue with you about what we should do."

"Good thinking. But what…are we doing?"

He drove. "I'm working on it."

ROYAL DROVE WITHOUT a full idea of what his destination was. He had to work out what had just happened.

There would have been more blood inside his apartment. Not his. Not Franny's. That was something. But why blood at all?

He thought about the splintering on Franny's door frame. It had been obvious—maybe not to a layman, but someone had to know she had police protection. The break-in at his place was way less obvious, the smear of blood inconsequential. He wouldn't have noticed it if he hadn't been looking because of *Franny's* apartment.

He couldn't help but wonder if it had all been a kind of trap. That he was *meant* to notice Franny's place had been compromised. Rush to his and…

Something bad was inside. He knew that without going in. But what he wasn't sure of was the purpose. A threat? Maybe he should have checked it out, but with Franny…

No, best to leave to someone else. Beckett could handle it. Royal had to admit he was coming around to trusting Beckett.

"Mr. Simmons is going to check the security," Franny said, reading from her phone. "I gave him permission to access all the footage. He'll text me back when he's gotten something. Copeland, on the other hand…"

"Wants us to come into the station," he finished for her. No surprises there.

"Yeah."

Maybe it was best. Maybe it only felt wrong because of

his old gang-member, knee-jerk responses, but the sheriff wanting to pull Franny's security still irked. Going back to a place where they thought she should be *fine* whether they knew if the kidnapper was in jail or not felt wrong.

Still, she'd be safe there. Surrounded by cops and all those detectives she knew. If he dropped her there, slipped away to handle this…she'd be safe. Beckett could make sure of it. He glanced at her as he drove down the mostly empty highway in the opposite direction of Bent.

She lifted her gaze to meet his. Her eyes were full of trust. And panic, but underneath that panic and worry was *trust*. He didn't deserve it.

But her words from this morning kept coming back to him. How much belief and trust she had in him. No, she didn't know his past.

But she did know his present. And she was so…smart. So intuitive. Couldn't he trust her instincts better than his own?

Maybe he didn't deserve her trust, her belief, her thinking he was good or brave, but maybe… Maybe he could be all those things because she *did* think them of him.

Maybe he had to be.

"It's not a bad idea to go to the police station," he said, his voice gruff. "The sheriff won't be able to ignore the fact someone broke into your place. That's a crime. You could officially report it, and we could just…stay put until we have more information."

He glanced in the rearview mirror, ready to make a U-turn on the highway, head back to Bent and trust the establishment he'd bought into when he became a cop. How was he ever supposed to move forward if he was still thinking like a scared teenager who couldn't trust anyone or any system?

That wasn't why he'd stayed put near Brooke, his only

family. That wasn't why he'd gotten through the police academy or applied at Bent. He'd taken all those steps as part of an acceptance that he was an adult now. He had the power, and he wanted to use that power to help where he could—in a way that mattered.

Good and brave.

But he caught a flash of another car in that rearview mirror. He might not have thought anything of it, but a car that same color silver had pulled onto the highway as he'd left Hope Town proper. He thought it had turned off back at the exit to Bent County, but it was still there.

Far enough away to be a tail.

Or it's a different car, or some old lady driving at the speed of molasses. Don't jump to conclusions. This isn't the Sons.

Since the coast was clear, he made the U-turn. If that person followed them back the other direction, then he'd know for sure. And if they did—he'd be headed to the police station. If they didn't, well, he was getting Franny to safety either way.

Franny's phone pinged. "It's another text from Copeland. He says, 'Second thought, don't come to the police station. Dead body of kidnapper found.'" Franny looked up at him wide-eyed.

"Well, we're good then. He's dead and we're on our way to the station. You can ID him and..."

Franny cleared her throat. "There's more, Royal." Her voice shook. "They found the body...in your apartment."

Yeah, definitely not good.

Chapter Twenty-One

Franny had managed to settle her panic a bit, until the last part of that text. Why would the dead body of the kidnapper be in *Royal's* apartment? She knew her writer brain wasn't based in reality, but the only thing that made any kind of sense to her was that…

"Someone…set you up?"

"Maybe."

He was so calm. So detached. "What do you mean, maybe?" she demanded, unable to be any of those things. "There's a dead body in your apartment. *You* didn't put it there."

"No," he agreed easily.

"Royal."

He flicked a glance at her, but there was nothing behind it. No heat or ice or anything. Just a kind of blankness that chilled her. "I'm going to take you to the police station."

"No, we're not going anywhere near the police station. Copeland told us not to." She waved her phone at him as if that would get through to him. "We're going to listen."

"I'll just drop you off."

"Royal." She couldn't let him do that, but she couldn't quite think of what to say that might get through that *cop* facade. She'd seen Copeland and Thomas put that on. So easily shutting off any...*person* underneath this job they did. The only thing she could do when they did that was maintain being reasonable. Find some cop facade of her own.

"I understand you think getting me out of the way would be safe," she said, hoping her voice sounded as calm as his. "But Copeland is telling us to stay away. *Us.* We need to listen to him, so we don't complicate whatever they need to investigate with the..."

"The dead man in my apartment?" he replied blandly, but she *saw* the flicker of irritation. Whether at her or the murder she wasn't sure, but emotion felt like progress.

Before she could continue to convince him they needed to turn back around and head away from Hope Town *and* Bent, he swore viciously.

He was glaring at the road, so Franny looked out. There was a car on the opposite side coming toward them. Why did it look familiar? But she couldn't consider that, because she realized the car was not driving on its side of the street.

"Royal, is that car..." The car kept going *faster*, and it was *clearly* in their lane, heading right toward them.

"Hold on, Franny."

She gripped the door, because there was no way that car was not careening right toward them. She squeezed her eyes shut, braced for some kind of impact even as Royal jerked the wheel and tried to avoid the collision.

But she felt the impact, the sound of crunching metal and shattering glass exploding around her as the car seemed to move at a completely bizarre angle. Franny jerked against her seatbelt at the impact, but holding on to the door and the odd angle of the force of collision kept her from bashing her head against anything.

But they kept...moving. Spinning? Something hit the back of her head, but it was all kind of surreal. She tried to open her eyes, but the force of everything made it impossible to do anything but tense her entire body and wait for it all to be over.

Finally, the car stopped moving. Once she realized that, Franny opened her eyes. They'd twisted around so they were facing the wrong way. The collision must have happened to the back end of the car because the front end looked perfectly fine. Which meant they were okay. They could be okay even though the airbags hadn't gone off.

She frowned at that. They should have, shouldn't they? That had been a hell of a jolt, even if it had been to the back of the car. Oh well, as long as they were okay.

"Roy—" She looked toward him. He was crumpled over the steering wheel.

He wasn't moving.

Panic speared through her, and she lunged for him, but she was held in place by the seatbelt. "Royal. Royal. *Royal!*" She slapped at her seatbelt, desperate to get it off, to get over to him. He wasn't moving.

Why hadn't any airbags gone off? Why wasn't he *moving*?

She managed to get the seatbelt out of her way, but now that she'd had enough time to think, she was scared to try to move him. What if he'd hurt his neck or spine? If she moved him to see what was wrong, she'd make it worse. Wouldn't she?

She wouldn't let her mind go there. "It's okay, Royal. It's okay. It's going to be okay." She said it more for her benefit than his, because it kept the panic from turning into hysterics.

She fumbled with her phone. Since her text to Copeland was still open on the screen, she just hit the call button at the top. He'd have a better idea of where they were to send help rather than trying to explain her location to a 911 dispatcher.

With shaking hands and her teeth chattering, she reached out with her free hand and grabbed Royal's wrist. She knew how to find a pulse, and a pulse would mean everything could be okay.

"Franny? I can't talk right now."

"Cope…" She thought she felt a pulse. Didn't she? The steady thump of life? Or was she hallucinating?

Copeland's voice in her ear was kind of a buzz.

"We…had an accident." She was pretty sure she got those words out. It was weird. She didn't think she'd hit her head, but it was kind of aching now. And her words didn't…sound right.

She sucked in a breath, trying to focus. Royal needed help. He had a pulse. She was *determined* he had a pulse. So she needed help.

But before she could manage to put those words together, the passenger door flung open. A woman stood there. For a blinding moment of pure hope, Franny thought they were saved.

Then she saw the woman's sharp smile and remembered that a car had been careening *at* them. And if it hadn't been someone's medical event that led to the dangerous speed and direction, it had been done very much on purpose.

Considering there was a dead body in Royal's apartment, well….

"God, this couldn't be more perfect." The woman laughed, actually *laughed*. "Well, F.M. Perkins, come on out. We've got places to go."

She must not have seen the phone in Franny's hand. Franny's body and face might be blocking it. For a moment of pure adrenaline and clarity, Franny knew that she would need her phone.

She swallowed, angling her body even farther and doing everything she could to shove the phone—the call with Copeland still going—into her pocket without the woman seeing.

"Damn, that's a hell of a party trick," the woman said, which made absolutely no sense to Franny. The woman must have read that in her expression. "You've got a shard of glass really lodged in there." She said, pointing at the back of Franny's head.

The pain in her head. A shard of glass? She reached up with a shaky hand.

"I wouldn't. Gonna hurt like hell. Besides, we've got places to be," the woman said, she patted her hip and that's when Franny realized she had a gun in a holster. "Out of the car now."

Franny didn't know what else to do but obey. Royal no doubt had a gun on that belt of his, but she could hardly get to it, get it *out* of the belt, *and* shoot it in any defensive fashion before this woman shot her.

And if the woman shot her, what might she do to Royal?

So Franny got out of the car. Help was coming. Copeland would get help. Everything would be okay if she could keep this all from…escalating.

She winced and tried not to groan in pain, but for as much as she thought she'd managed to not get hurt since she wasn't unconscious, everything screamed in protest at moving.

Especially her head. Every move, every step sent a searing, slicing pain down the back of her skull. She lifted her hand again but was a little too afraid to try to touch anything. A shard of glass *stuck* in there sounded…really bad.

The woman—and it had to be the woman Royal had seen poking around Hope Town in the beginning of this. What had he said her name was? Holand something.

So, this was the former FBI agent, somehow connected to Albennie. But why was she after Franny? Why… She swallowed at the lump in her throat as she thought of Royal slumped in that car. He needed medical attention. They needed help.

She hoped and prayed that came across to Copeland.

"We're just going to get a ways off this road here. So no one sees us before I'm ready. You go on and walk ahead of me. You try to run—well that glass will probably stop you, but a bullet will too."

Franny took a staggering step forward. She tried to walk softly and slowly as much to delay any possible harm until help got there as because of the pain. But the waves of pain just throbbed through every inch of her until tears were filling her eyes. She couldn't think straight from all the hurt, except to move forward one excruciating step at a time.

She *felt* the woman walking behind her. She wasn't holding the gun. It was just in a holster at her hip. Maybe Franny could run…or fight, but the thought of trying to do either with this horrific pain in her head kept her from actually trying.

She didn't know how long they walked. Into the trees. Oh, she shouldn't have come this far. But what else was there to do? The woman had a gun. Royal needed help. What was she supposed to *do*?

With no warning, something…happened to the back of her head. She screamed out in pain, her hand flying instinctually up to the source. Her hand came away wet with blood. She stared at the woman who now held the bloody shard of glass that had been *in her head.*

Holand must have yanked it out.

Franny's vision wavered and she couldn't stay upright. She managed not to fully pass out. Just kind of crumpled to her hands and knees, nausea sweeping through her. She breathed raggedly, staring at the ground where tears and blood dripped.

"Yeah, why don't you pass out?" Holand said. "That'd make this a lot easier on all of us now that we're here."

But Franny had to breathe through the pain. Stay awake. It was her only chance. Royal's only chance.

She could feel the blood dripping down the back of her neck. Oh God, maybe neither of them had any kind of chance.

"Now, we're going to have to make this look a little bit more…believable." She cocked her head to one side, studying Franny. "The glass is clearly from the accident, so we need a struggle. Don't we?"

Then, without any kind of warning, she lifted her foot and kicked hard into Franny's side so Franny fell over. The shock of the blow elicited another howl of pain, but as the woman was gripping her shirt and tearing it, Franny fought back.

She kicked out herself, she wriggled, she pushed. It was instinct beyond avoiding pain. Not letting this woman hurt her any more than she was already hurt. The screaming agony in her head was a distraction, but it didn't make her *stop* fighting back. But there was so little she could do.

She managed to get on her butt and scoot back, but the woman was getting to her feet, brushing the dirt off her clothes.

"There we go. Now we've got a struggle."

Franny looked down at herself. Her shirt was bloody

and torn. There were scrapes on her hands. Dirt all over her pants.

"What are you doing? Why?" Franny demanded, because everything just hurt, and she couldn't tell if the liquid on her cheeks was blood or tears or both. She was so baffled and just hurting.

"Look, you learn a lesson real quick in the real world. You can't trust a man as far as you can throw him. If there's any complaint I have about your books, it's that one."

"You… My *books*?"

"Sure, had to do some research on the witness, didn't I? They're not half bad. I have some critiques, but they pass an evening all right. Except for the idea that there are *heroes* in this world, F.M. But I guess that's why it's classified fiction."

Franny could only gape at this woman. Discussing the believability of her *books* while Royal was unconscious, and she was bleeding at an alarming rate. This woman had *crashed into them* and she had *critiques*.

"In the *real* world, there are the users and the used. You gotta be smart enough to be a user. I used Tony for what he was good for, and when he couldn't do that right?" She shrugged. "Well, collateral damage is a term for a reason. You see, I'm a pretty good writer too. I've got all sorts of ideas. So, we're working this story out. Brainstorm with me."

Franny stared up at her. Did any of those words make sense? If they did, maybe she had a worse head injury than she thought.

"So, the police will come upon the scene I left for them. The second scene. They'll blame your cop boyfriend for Tony, the first scene, since the body was in his place. But you saw the cop off Tony. Oh no! He's got to get rid of you too. He drives you out to the middle of nowhere. He's dragging you out of the car. Here because he thinks the bears will get you and he won't have to explain *your* body. In his head, he'll get back to take care of Tony before the cops know the difference."

Franny looked around. Sure there were bears in Bent County, but she didn't think one happening upon her dead body was much of a plan for body removal.

And why was she actually considering this like a *book*, when this was her *life*?

"But I happen to drive by," Holand continued, really getting into it. "I see him. Hero that I am, because it's fiction, right? But even in real life stupid people want to believe in heroes. I run into his car to stop him. But it's too late. I call the police, then disappear. Neat and tidy like. We all win. How's that for a happy ending? If I didn't have to kill you, I'd let you write that one. Your books aren't bad. Could use an editor."

Franny was almost positive this had to be a very lucid dream. But she didn't wake up. No reality came calling. She sat there on the ground, *bleeding*, and stared at this woman. "No one would ever believe any of that. In real life *or* in one of my books. There's a million plot holes."

The satisfied look on the woman's face turned into a scowl. "Says you."

"Says…reason and rationality. Royal is still in the car. He hasn't moved. How did he kill me then crawl back into the crashed-out car? He's *unconscious*." She forced herself to add the next bit even though she didn't want to say it out loud. "He might be *dead*."

The woman lifted her chin. "I've got that figured out. Don't you worry about it." She flashed a smug smile again.

"I won't. But you should worry about this. The police

know who you are. They all know who you are, *Holand.* So you can run, but you can't disappear. They're already looking for you. Thanks to Royal."

Franny had a glimmer of satisfaction as the smile slid off the woman's face. The woman stood very still. Enough of a moment that Franny felt a bubble of hope.

But then the woman shrugged. "That's a shame. Because if I can't frame him, I don't have time to mess around with you." And as she raised the gun, Franny realized she'd made a fatal mistake.

ROYAL CAME TO on a stab of pain and a wave of nausea. He coughed, pain wracking his system. Something came out of his mouth when he coughed.

Blood.

Hell.

"Franny?" he croaked. He managed to lift his head, even though it hurt worse than he'd ever been hurt—and he'd been beaten and shot and all manner of things.

Her seat was empty, her door open. She must have gone to get help. That was good. He could just…rest until help came.

He managed to sit up, sort of, lean his head back. Sunlight gleamed off the car and it hurt his head. He closed his eyes, and closing his eyes seemed to help steady his jumbled thoughts.

He swore.

That hadn't just been some car accident. Someone had hit them on purpose. He'd tried to swerve out of the way, but he hadn't been willing to risk Franny, so he'd swerved in the only way he could to keep his side of the car the target.

The airbags hadn't gone off. That was…wrong. Someone had to have messed with his car.

Everything was wrong.

Which meant Franny likely hadn't gone for help. She'd likely been taken by whoever had crashed into them.

He heard a sound. Turned his head toward it. The passenger door was open. Someone was out there. The car that had rammed into him was there in the road, and someone was out beyond the road. In the trees.

He had to get out. Find Franny. He had to… He looked down at his uniform. His walkie wasn't turned on, but he was wearing it.

Gritting his teeth together, he lifted his hand to turn it on. He was greeted by the steady sounds of radio traffic and the occasional burst of static. With what little strength he seemed to have, he managed to depress the talk button. He croaked out his department serial number, and his location, best as he could remember it. "Car accident."

He needed them to know it was dangerous though. No accident. Who had been the driver of the car if the kidnapper was dead in his apartment?

The only other person he'd been looking into. Holand Meyer. He managed to give a description. Or thought he did.

"Units have already been dispatched, Deputy Campbell," the dispatcher said. "ETA is a few minutes."

Already been dispatched? How? Had someone seen something?

It didn't matter. A few minutes was still too long if Franny wasn't *here*. Ignoring the rest of the radio noise, he put all his focus on getting his door open. It didn't go at first. Most of the damage had been done to the back end of the car, but enough that it made his door stuck.

He had to fight it, and the pain, and every other damn thing, but he finally wrenched it open. He was having a hard time breathing. Probably a cracked rib. Maybe worse. Couldn't think about it. Had to stay conscious and find Franny.

He managed to get out, get to his feet, and then he had to lean against the car, close his eyes, breathe. Just breathe. It wasn't just the hurting. He was dizzy, nauseated. Rough shape. Maybe he should just wait for backup.

Then he heard that sound again. Someone in pain.

Franny.

He pushed himself off the car and started walking for the trees. His vision was blurry, but he just kept moving by sheer force of will.

He fumbled with the latch on his holster but finally got it free and got the gun out. His left arm screamed in pain no matter how he moved it, but he gripped the gun in his right and kept moving.

He just had to stay conscious long enough to stop the threat. Hell, he could *die* after that, which felt like a real possibility at the moment.

Gun in one hand, he tried to use the other hand to lean against a tree, get his bearings, but his arm screamed in pain at any pressure put on it.

Not good. None of this was *good.*

He thought he'd spared Franny the worst of the accident, but what if he hadn't? He had to find her.

He blew out a breath, concentrated on getting his eyes to focus while he ignored his body. He'd had to learn, hadn't he? Pain didn't matter. Pain was weakness. You had to ignore the pain. To survive. Survive. *Survive.*

He was so damn sick of surviving. So tired of everything hurting. Pain and suffering and the whims of horrible people ruining *everything.* He'd been fighting it for so long, why did he keep doing it?

Because there'd always been a voice in the back of his head. Brooke's voice, urging him to be better, do some good.

But Brooke was well and taken care of and what did *he* matter anymore?

Franny.

She was out there. All because she'd *seen* someone do something bad and tried to stop it. He couldn't let her be another horrible person's victim. She deserved more than survival.

Hell, they all did.

She thought he was brave and good, no matter what he'd told her. She'd held on to that belief, so he had to hold on to it now.

Something was going to change after this. He didn't have the presence of mind to know what just yet, but once he could think, once he could *breathe* without this searing pain, he was going to figure it out.

He kept moving forward, trying to be quiet, but with the agony radiating through his body and the odd drumming in his ears, he didn't know for sure if he was being stealthy or as subtle as a Mack truck.

There were tracks in the dirt. Not clear ones, but indentations in the dry ground, the sweep of dried pine needles moved by someone's footsteps.

The occasional drop of blood. He followed them, focusing only on finding Franny and nothing going on in his own body.

He thought he heard voices, so he stopped, tried to focus his vision. In the distance, between trees, he saw a flash of something. He didn't know what, so he just kept moving for it.

After a few more yards, he could make out the scene clearly.

The woman he'd seen skulking around Hope Town stood, gun in hand, back to him. She wasn't a brunette now, but a blonde. Franny sat, bloody and dirty. Royal couldn't quite make out what they were saying—not because they were far away or quiet, but because his ears were just kind of a low buzz.

But Holand Meyer didn't turn around to face him, so she must not know he was there, but he saw what was coming the moment Franny did. Her eyes went wide. And that was enough to have Holand turning, gun in hand, raised to aim at him.

Royal didn't wait, didn't think. He just lifted his own gun and shot.

Of course, so did she.

The force of the bullet hit him dead center. And he fell back, which hurt more than the bullet to his vest.

His *vest*. He wanted to laugh, might have if he wasn't in so much damn pain.

Being a cop had saved him after all.

Chapter Twenty-Two

Franny raced forward on an outraged cry. She'd shot Royal. She'd shot him. He'd fallen over and *oh God*, *oh God*. Franny wouldn't let her shoot again.

But there was nothing to be done because Holand was also on the ground. She was bleeding. It seeped out of her side. Franny stood above her, watching her move and writhe. For a moment, Franny did nothing but stare, a bit like she'd been detached from her own body.

Royal had shot Holand too. She was *shot*. She didn't even have her gun anymore. But Franny realized that's where Holand's eyes were trained. The gun a few feet away from her outstretched hand.

Her whole body shaking, Franny managed to grab it before Holand could wriggle close enough to. Then she rushed over to Royal, stumbled onto her knees by his side. His eyes were closed.

"Royal."

"It's too damn bright out here," he muttered.

Oh, *God*, he'd spoken. He'd spoken. He was still alive. He was… "I thought she killed you," Franny managed to choke out.

"Vest. Hell of a thing."

Everything fell apart then. He had a vest on because and

only because he was in uniform. He wasn't dead. Oh, he was so hurt, but he wasn't dead. She simply lowered her forehead to said vest and wept into it.

She felt a hand on her shoulder and whirled, ready to fight or shoot or whatever she had to do.

But it was Copeland. A few deputies. Copeland easily swiped the gun out of her hand.

"Damn, Franny, you're bleeding like hell. We need to get you to a hospital too." He looked over at some people, shouted orders.

"I'm okay. I'm better than he is. She shot him. She *shot* him. Copeland, you have to..."

Some EMTs rushed over with a stretcher. They talked to each other as they worked to get Royal moved onto it.

Copeland helped her to her feet, and out of the way. He held her in one place while deputies and EMTs swarmed the area. She wanted to be with Royal. She wanted...so many things, but her mind couldn't seem to make a decision.

Except... She had the truth. Answers. Sort of. She looked up at Copeland helplessly.

"Copeland, she told me everything. I mean, not *why*, but...that she killed the kidnapper. That she was framing Royal. She was going to frame him for me too, but the story didn't make sense."

"We'll take your statement once you're checked out," Copeland said gently. "I'm sure it'll corroborate whatever angle the damn Feds are working from." The EMTs were moving Royal, and Franny took a step toward him, but Copeland held firm.

"You can't go with him, Franny. Hey, Bowman. Come check her out, huh?"

Another EMT came over, had Franny sit down on the ground. "I'll clean this up and get a bandage on it, but she's going to need to be transported too."

"I'm fine."

Both the EMT and Copeland gave her a disapproving look.

"We'll get another ambulance here soon as we can. She'll hold up all right," the EMT said. She could feel his hands on her hair and she winced.

The pain she'd nearly forgotten in all her fear and panic was back, tenfold, throbbing through her body like a drumbeat. She was so, so tired all of a sudden that the EMT had to hold her up.

She looked up at where Copeland stood, still coordinating everything with that blank cop mask on.

"Copeland, it's over now, right?"

He looked down at her, a flicker of emotion in his gaze now. Sympathy. Relief. "Yeah, Franny. It's over."

THE BEEPING WAS going to drive him insane.

It was the first coherent thought Royal'd had in what felt like a very long time. When he blinked his eyes open, nothing fully made sense except if that beeping didn't stop he was going to…

Well, not a whole lot because he couldn't seem to move the way he wanted to. He could turn his head, and when he did, he came face-to-face with his sister.

"Chick." His voice sounded rough.

Brooke smiled, but she'd been crying. It was all over her face. Red eyes and puffy cheeks. "You're really getting shot way too much for my personal comfort."

"Had a vest this time."

"Thank God."

He tried to shift in the bed, but he didn't feel in control of his limbs just yet, and he realized one of said limbs was in a cast. His left arm. He stared at it, not fully making sense of it. A broken arm. Must have been from the accident.

Accident. "Franny?"

"She's doing all right. They stitched her up. She had to stay overnight, but they released her today. Just a nasty gash on her head, but otherwise she's fine." Brooke scooted closer to the bed, peering at him. "She's waiting to see you. Refuses to leave until they let her. They were only letting family sit with you while you were coming out of the anesthesia."

"She should go."

Brooke frowned. "She wants to see you. Why should she go?"

He had answers for that, but he couldn't seem to find them in the swimming feeling in his brain. "Am I dying or something?"

"No. Broken nose, broken arm, concussion, bruised and cracked ribs, honestly too many bumps, bruises and lacerations to count, but you're going to be okay. If I have to personally see to it."

"You need to take care of yourself, Chick." She was *pregnant*. She shouldn't be worrying over him. She didn't say anything to that, just frowned disapprovingly at him.

Royal sighed. It hurt, but not the way it *had*. Pain killers, probably. Or that anesthesia Brooke was talking about. How long had he been out of it? He kind of remembered arriving, but everything around that was a blur.

One thing was clear though. "I wasn't fast enough. Not the first time. Couldn't get the car out of the way. I should have seen it coming. I should have *known*."

Brooke studied him for a long time, that serious study that always felt like she saw more than he'd ever understand. She brushed at the hair on his forehead, like she had when he'd been a little kid. Before they'd been separated.

"You are incredibly brave, Royal. A hero. The people you've saved in your life would have *died* otherwise. So you don't get to be hard on yourself."

He didn't argue with her. He *wanted* to, but he supposed now wasn't the time.

Hero? With them all beat up like this? He didn't think so.

But he heard Franny's words in his head. *You cannot tell me you aren't good or brave, because that is the heart of who you are. Period.*

Brooke stood. "I'm going to go get Franny."

"What if I don't want you to?" He had things to work out, and he wasn't strong enough to stand up to how much he wanted… So much he wanted…

"You're wrong," Brooke said simply. "And you'll have to tell *her* that. I'd suggest not." She swept out of the room. Mad at him. Which wasn't fair.

He didn't think.

Didn't matter. He had to think of the right words to get Franny to leave, and his brain wasn't firing on all cylinders, so it'd be a challenge.

She came in, clasping her hands together. She had a bandage wrapped around her head, and the clothes she was wearing were too big for her, clearly not hers. Hers had been ripped and bloody.

He could see her there. On the ground. It gripped him, all that fear sweeping through him again even as she moved across the room to hover over his bed, cleaned up, bandaged up and okay.

He'd been so sure he'd tell her to go away. To give him space. He couldn't get the words out, because just looking at her made everything okay.

"Hi," she said. Her green eyes were shiny with tears.

"Hi," he managed, wanting to take those tears away.

But she smiled. It wobbled, but it was a smile. "I… I don't know how much Brooke told you, but Holand made it through surgery. She's going to go away for a very long time. The Feds still won't give a lot of details, but basically this woman has been a kind of informant of sorts, using her inside FBI knowledge to work for hire. The group that kidnapped Albennie hired Holand to find her, then *she* hired the kidnapper. I haven't talked to Mr. Simmons yet—he'll probably have more information—but it seems like everyone involved at every step is now in jail."

Royal didn't really understand the words—he'd blame all the drugs in his system for now, but she just kept talking, standing there, hands clasped. Nervous and upset.

He'd been so sure this was it. He'd put a wall up. Look what had happened to her in just a few days of being involved with him? He was bad luck. A harbinger.

But she just babbled on about everything that had happened. How many stitches she'd gotten, how many times Rosalie had thrown up in the waiting room. Such silly little details and he just…couldn't stand the thought of suddenly not having Franny in his life.

He didn't want to be bad luck anymore.

He wanted…a future. To be the brave and the good she saw. Wasn't that why he'd become a cop? Wasn't that why he'd stayed here in Bent County? A future meant believing he deserved one. He didn't deserve her.

But he'd work at it.

She sat abruptly in the chair Brooke had vacated, looked pained. "I'm probably giving you a headache."

But she wasn't. "I like hearing your voice."

Her mouth curved and she leaned forward, touching a spot on his forehead. "I like seeing your eyes open."

For a few quiet moments, they just stared at each other, maybe reassuring themselves the other was all right.

"When I'm on my own two feet again. And you don't have that bandage on your head. We're going to go out."

She blinked once. "Out?"

"To dinner. A movie. Whatever. A date." He tried to move, winced when it hurt. "Like normal people."

"A date?" she repeated.

"Yes," he said firmly.

"Oh. Well, okay."

"You want to, don't you?" he demanded.

She was looking at him with serious green eyes. "Yes. Though I don't know how normal I can be. But I can try."

He laughed. It hurt. But somehow that was…just right now too. "Well, okay then. That's what we'll do. But don't try to be normal. Just be you."

"I think that's a compliment," she grumbled. "Are you sure you're not delusional?" she asked, leaning forward. "Hyped up on pain killers and anesthesia. You might change your mind."

He stared at her. After everything, all this, his whole damn life, she still made him smile. "I'm sure. I won't. I like having you in my life, Franny."

She swallowed hard. "You're a real hero, Royal."

Well, it wasn't going to be easy. He shifted, winced at the pain. "I don't know about all that."

"I do. That Holand woman… She said heroes are fictional. But she's wrong. Maybe heroes aren't all perfectly good, but there *are* heroes." Her eyes filled with tears again, but they still didn't fall. "People who do the right thing in the face of bad things, hard things. That's you."

He didn't want to believe it, but Brooke had said it. Franny had said it. How could he argue with two of the best, strongest women he knew?

"Well, then it's you too, Franny."

She looked puzzled for a minute, then straightened her shoulders. "You know what? I'll take it."

He managed a little bit of a laugh, even if it hurt.

Maybe he'd learn to take it too. With her.

Epilogue

Three Months Later

Franny was in the bakery talking to Albennie and Lia over coffee, marveling inwardly at how much Albennie looked like her old self. Even though she'd only been kidnapped a few days, she'd come back looking skinny and haunted.

These days, she looked like she had before. Strong and sure and happy.

She didn't talk about the kidnapping, and the police still only knew that whatever Albennie had been involved in was related to a federal case, but the people who'd wanted her were all behind bars. Where they belonged.

As long as she was safe, that was what mattered.

So life was good, and Franny knew how to appreciate that. Especially with her book almost done.

The bell on the door jangled and all three women looked to see Royal striding in. He wasn't in uniform, but he had his serious cop expression on.

"God, he's hot," Albennie muttered before he made it over to them.

"I know," Franny said with a grin. "And all mine." He even spent most nights at her place now. He volunteered for the Hope Town sector whenever he had the chance.

Three months had been exactly what Franny had always hoped a real, adult relationship might be like. Not perfect, not always romantic. Solid. Real. Nothing she could write in a book because it was cooking meals together or drinking their coffee or arguing on which team had the better starting rotation.

They were building something like her cousins had with their significant others, and that filled Franny with all kinds of hope.

"Bragger," Lia muttered. "Except who wants a cop?"

Before Franny could answer that, Royal linked his arm with hers. No greeting. Just: "We have to go."

"Where?" she asked as he pulled her along, a little worry fluttering low in her stomach.

"Brooke's having the baby."

"Oh!" Worry turned to excitement. Except…she shouldn't be coming with. She'd spent more time with Brooke and Zeke since she and Royal had been dating, but this was still…a family thing.

"Brooke probably doesn't want non-family in her hospital room. It's a sacred place, Royal."

"Zeke said it was okay. His brother and sister are going to be there with their kids and everything. I can't face a baby *alone*, Franny. She's going to want me to hold it."

"Him, Royal. The baby is a boy."

"Right, right. See, that's why I need you." She liked seeing him flustered, because he only ever was about truly wonderful things. And she thought…maybe someday they'd get to a point where good things and babies and building families didn't fluster him so much, and she wanted to be around to see that.

Maybe she had lots of dreams about the future, but she didn't need everything to happen at once or quickly. In fact, it was nice to just enjoy dating somebody. While Rosalie grew her baby, and Audra planned her wedding, Franny was getting to know her boyfriend.

And apparently his new nephew.

ROYAL WAS GLAD he'd dragged Franny along, because he didn't know what the hell he was supposed to do in the waiting room, waiting for updates. But Franny chatted with Zeke's family and in-laws. She entertained Zeke's brother's toddler and had a very serious discussion about Taylor Swift with his brother-in-law's teenager.

Because she just had a *way* about her.

When Zeke came out to the waiting room, everyone was desperate for an update. "Baby's here," he said, raking a hand through his hair like he couldn't quite believe he'd said those words. "Brooke's…amazing. Everything's great. She wants to see Royal first." Zeke looked as unsteady and winded as Royal had ever seen him—and he'd seen him face down men with guns. "You come on too, Franny. We'll do the families one at a time."

Royal didn't stiffen at the word *families* like he once had. Maybe Franny wasn't his family, but he liked where they were going. And luckily, in the moment, he could focus more on other people's babies than his own stuff.

Zeke led them down a hall and into a room. Royal immediately crossed to his sister sitting in the hospital bed, a little bundle wrapped in her arms.

Everything that had been stacked against them from the start didn't matter now. She'd brought life into this world. His sister was a mother, and he knew she'd be the best one in the world.

Brooke smiled at him, tears in her eyes. "Well, hello, Uncle Royal."

"Heya, Chick." He pressed an uncharacteristic kiss to her

forehead, relieved she looked happy and whole. He peered down at the little baby and its—*his*—red and scrunched-up face.

"Royal."

He looked back at Franny's tight voice. She was looking at some little card on the bassinet thingy. He squinted at the card. It read *It's A Boy*, and then underneath had all the pertinent details written out.

Like name. "Campbell Royal Daniels." He looked back at his sister, emotion clogging his throat. "Hell, Chick. What did you do that for?"

"Because our names mean something. Something good now. Because we fought for it. And I hope he never has to fight for *anything*," she said, looking down at the tiny baby in her arms. "But if he does, he'll have some fine examples." She smiled up at him, tears glimmering in her eyes. "Now sit down so you can hold him."

"I told you she'd make me," Royal muttered to Franny as they moved over to a little bench under the window. He was unsteady, unmoored and so…damn happy.

Yeah, their names meant something now. Something good. Something brave.

Zeke brought the bundle over and Franny instructed Royal how to hold his arms. The baby was so tiny. A little fluff of nothing. And yet the biggest, brightest thing in the world. His little nephew.

"Oh, Brooke, isn't he just the handsomest little thing?" Franny said, running a finger along one of the little wrinkles on his forehead.

"Yes," Brooke said emphatically.

They stayed a little while. Royal was happy to hand the baby back to Brooke. He was determined to be a damn good uncle and involved as hell, but…maybe a little less hands on until the baby firmed up a little bit.

He walked out of the hospital hand in hand with Franny. "Thanks for coming with me. The moral support was appreciated. But now you have to be there every time I'm forced to hold him before he gets old enough for that not to be terrifying."

She smiled at him. "Anytime."

They reached his car, but he didn't let her go. In the fading autumn light, he kept her hand in his. She looked up at him quizzically.

There were better ways to do it, to say it, but it was this moment that gave him the courage he'd been lacking for a while now. That his sister had built a family. That he'd… come to this moment. Where he had a life and some peace and too much good to deserve.

But that just meant he had to take it. "Franny, I love you."

She looked up at him, didn't say anything right away. Sometimes he thought he knew exactly what was going on in her head, and sometimes he didn't have a clue.

As the silence stretched out, he didn't have a damn clue. Especially when a little nervous flutter started up in his chest.

"Well?" he finally demanded, because what the hell? Why had he done this in a hospital parking lot? He should have planned it out. He should have… Made sure she was going to say something *back*.

But she just stared at him. "Well what?"

"Aren't you going to say something?"

She inhaled, then slowly let the breath out, still staring at him with all that vibrant green. "I was trying to think of…the right thing to say."

"It's pretty damn simple, isn't it?"

"Yes, and no." She reached up, put her hands on his

cheeks, like she was about to let him down gently, and he didn't know what the hell to do with *that*.

Well, he'd… He'd figure out a way to fix it. He could be patient. Maybe she wasn't ready yet, and that was okay. It would be okay. He'd *make* it okay.

"You are my hero," she said very seriously.

"I hate it when you say that," he muttered, trying to move his head out of her grasp, but she held firm.

"I know. But I don't think you'll hate this. I love you too, Royal." She pushed up onto her toes and pressed her mouth to his. It was a sweet kiss, and he could have deepened it, but… He pulled away.

"What the hell did you put me through the ringer for?"

She laughed, and he loved the sound of it. Loved *her*. Even if she had just about scared him to death.

"I wasn't *trying* to. I was trying to enjoy the moment. Commit it to memory. *Savor*."

He grunted in irritation, but she kept her arms around his neck and that wasn't irritating at all.

"Just think, when Campbell is like fifteen, I'll be able to say, your uncle told me he loved me for the first time the day you were born. And then, because he'll be a teenager, he'll be like, 'ew, gross, why would you tell me that?' And we'll both have a good laugh."

Royal couldn't imagine anything fifteen years down the line. Certainly not that little wisp of a baby being a teenage boy, but he liked the part where Franny was by his side still. Laughing.

Yeah, that was pretty much perfect.

* * * * *